STRIPPED AND BRANDED

A Yakima Henry Western

PETER BRANDVOLD

WOLFPACK PUBLISHING
— EST 2013 —

WOLFPACK PUBLISHING
— EST 2013 —

Paperback Edition
Copyright © 2021 Peter Brandvold

Published in the United States by Wolfpack Publishing, Las Vegas

Wolfpack Publishing
5130 S. Fort Apache Road, 215-380
Las Vegas, NV 89148

wolfpackpublishing.com

Paperback ISBN 978-1-64734-628-7
eBook ISBN 978-1-64734-627-0

STRIPPED AND BRANDED

Chapter 1

A man's yell rose above the storm's din.

"Helloo the camp! We're peaceable if you are an' that fire sure looks warm!"

Yakima smiled shrewdly and reached over to where his prized Yellowboy repeater leaned against the cave wall. He jacked a round into the chamber, off-cocked the hammer, then leaned the rifle against the log he was sitting on.

The fire danced in its blackened stone ring between him and the egg-shaped cave entrance. As it did, he stared out into the storm. His handsome, white-stockinged black stallion, Wolf, stood in the relative shelter of two large boulders and a wind-gnarled cedar about thirty feet down the slope beyond the cave.

Wolf turned to regard Yakima with his chocolate-dark eyes. The horse gave his tail one quick shake as though to say, "See?" Then, eyes still on Yakima, the black twitched first his left ear and then his right ear.

Again, Yakima smiled.

"How many are you?" he called into the buffeting gray veil of the rain.

Thunder had just peeled, sounding like a kettle drum, so he wondered if the man had heard him.

Then the voice came again from out in the high-mountain storm: "Just two of us! You got coffee on, partner?"

"Come in slow!" Yakima picked up the coffee cup he'd set down when the stallion had a minute ago alerted him to the presence of men on the lurk. The alert had been one soft whicker and a cautious glance at his rider. "Keep your hands where I can see 'em!"

"Like I said, we're peaceable!" came the yell again, from nearer this time.

A lightning bolt flashed wickedly over the top of the far, forest-carpeted ridge. Thunder crashed, making the ground shake.

Yakima stared through the pale smoke of the orange flames before him and presently spied movement on the slope below the cave and to the right of where he'd picketed the stallion. First one man appeared, hatted head-first and then the shoulders clad in a yellow rain slicker. He tramped up the slope with his head down, scowling at the discomfort of the storm, the rain sluicing down through the crease in his cream Stetson, obscuring his features. Saddlebags were draped over his left shoulder.

The second man appeared, walking a little behind and to the left of the first man, slumped under the weight of the saddle and bedroll on one shoulder and a pair of saddlebags on the other shoulder. The second man was taller than the first, thinner, and he wore a black Stetson.

"Whew!" said the shorter man as he approached the cave, ducking his head as he stepped through the opening, his baby blue eyes glistening orange in the light of the fire. "That smoke sure was a welcome smell when we was ridin' through, an' that coffee sure looks good!"

He glanced from Yakima to the cup in Yakima's left hand, the coal black brew lifting several tendrils of cream-colored steam.

The other, taller man had to duck even lower than the first man as he came through the cave entrance. He gave a strangled wail of discomfort and tossed his saddle and bedroll onto the ground. "Damn, that gets heavy!"

"Help yourself to the mud," Yakima said, studying both men closely as he sipped his own brew.

"Whew!" the taller man said again, dropping his saddlebags then doffing his black Stetson and running a gloved hand through his long, damp blond hair. "A real frog strangler!" he yowled, and grinned at Yakima. "Ain't that right, partner? A frog strangler an' gully washer!"

"No weather for men to be out in." Yakima glanced at the saddle. "Say, where's the horse that belongs to that saddle?"

The two men exchanged quick glances and then the smaller man—round-faced and almost baby-faced, probably in his mid- to late-twenties—dropped to his knees and laid his saddlebags out on the ground before him. "Damn rattler got Chet's appy. A real shame, too. It was a damn fine horse—wasn't it, Chet?"

"A damn fine one," Chet said, bending his long knees and shaking his head as he sat down beside his saddle and saddlebags, the worn brown leather beaded with moisture. "A real shame. I didn't see it until it struck. I don't think the damn thing even rattled." He looked at the shorter man, who was digging a tin cup out of a saddlebag pouch. "Did you hear it rattle, Tony?"

Tony shook his head as he grabbed the leather swatch Yakima had draped over a rock of the fire ring and used it to pluck the speckled black coffee pot off the iron spider. "No, I sure didn't. I thought they always rattled before they struck."

"That's a shame," Yakima said, again lifting his coffee to his lips. "Losing a good horse. I don't know what I'd do without that one there."

He glanced out the cave entrance at the black stallion who had his head turned so he could watch the goings-on in the cave, a skeptical cast to his round, dark eyes.

"Say, that's a fine black," Chet said, following Yakima's gaze to the horse. "Lean an' long-legged, deep-chested. I bet he can run all day and into tomorrow."

"He can at that. I don't know for sure, but I think he's got a little old Spanish in him, maybe some Arab. Been a good horse. We been together a long time."

"Fogged a few trails together—eh, amigo?" Chet said, holding his cup out as Tony filled it from the pot.

"A few," Yakima said.

Tony returned the pot to the spider and the leather swatch to the rock and glanced quickly at Yakima. "Just passin' through?"

"That's me. Always just passin' through." Yakima glanced at his two new camp partners just now making themselves comfortable on the other side of the fire. "You fellas, too? Or you work around here?"

Again, Chet and Tony shared a quick glance, not so much turning their heads but sliding their eyes—a furtive movement and with a little pink climbing into Tony's fair, cleanly shaven cheeks. "Yep, we sure do," he said. "Always pushin' cattle, don't ya know. From one meadow to another."

"Which outfit?"

Again, that quick flick of the newcomers' eyes.

Then Tony said, "Kitchen Sink," and quickly raised

his cup to his lips.

"Kitchen Sink," Yakima said, frowning and nodding slowly. "Who runs that these days? I used to know but my memory ain't as good as it once was. Is that run by Bruce Fairchild? That big fella from the Panhandle?"

Chat and Tony shared full-on glances now. Chuckling wryly, Chet, who was hatchet-faced and sporting several days of dark-brown beard stubble on his lean jaws, turned to Yakima and said, "Say, you're just full o' questions!"

Yakima hiked a shoulder. "Just makin' conversation. Oh, no—I got that wrong. Fairchild runs the Crosshatch. So...back to my original question"—he frowned curiously—"who runs the Kitchen Sink?"

Holding his steaming cup in both hands up close to his chin, he looked from Tony to Chet and back again, fashioning an affable smile to go with that curious frown. Chet and Tony stared back at him, their prior easy natures fading beneath a building cloud of suspicion.

"Don't worry about it," Chet said tonelessly over the rim of his own steaming cup.

"Just full o' questions," Tony said.

"Like I said," Yakima said. "Just makin' conversation. An' wonderin' who I'm sharin' my coffee with." He paused then continued with: "When I passed through Lone Pine a coupla days back, the bank had been robbed."

Tony frowned in surprise. "You don't say! Lone Pine,

huh?"

"Yep," Yakima said. "Lone Pine. Killed a couple of posse men."

Chet slid his eyes toward Tony. Tony kept his own gaze on Yakima, his blond brows forming a severe ridge above his eyes. "Takes all kinds," he said, softly.

"Don't it?" Yakima said.

"Did they catch the bank robbers?" Chet wanted to know.

"I haven't heard." Yakima sipped his coffee. "I rode out the next day."

"Hmmm," Tony said and gave his own coffee a tentative sip, sliding his quick glance toward Chet.

"How many were there?" Chet asked. "Bank robbers, I mean."

"Three. Wore masks so they wouldn't be identified."

"Hmm," Tony said, and nodded.

"Pretty desperate devils," Yakima said. "Real bad men."

"Takes all kinds, don't it?" Tony said and cast another of those, quick, furtive glances at his trail partner.

Outside the rain came down, the sound rising to a low roar. The coin-sized drops splashed on the wet ground. Thunder rumbled, occasionally banging loudly, like someone whacking an empty steel barrel with a heavy wooden stick. Witches' fingers of lightning sparked over the far ridge.

Inside the cave, the fire crackled and popped.

Keeping his gaze on Chet, Yakima said, "One had his horse shot out from under him."

"You don't say," Chet said.

"Yep."

"Cryin' shame," Tony said. "Shootin' a horse."

"I'd say worse than shootin' a man, but some would disagree," Yakima told him.

Tony gave a dry chuckle.

"He's prob'ly lookin' for a mount," Yakima said. "That horseless rider. Prob'ly slow-goin', ridin' double. I'm thinkin' maybe they forted up in one of these canyons out here between the Sangre de Cristos and the San Juans and are waitin' for an unsuspecting rider to happen along. Maybe a ranch hand from either the Kitchen Sink or the Crosshatch—two biggest ranches in these parts. Least-ways, they were the biggest spreads the last time I rode through here," he added.

Chet and Tony just stared at him over the leaping flames of the fire.

"Which one did you boys say you rode for?" Yakima asked them after nearly a minute of stony silence save the crackling fire and the thundering storm.

Nearly another minute of silence passed.

Chet and Tony both stared stonily at Yakima. Tony's fair-skinned face shown with a pink flush. He held his cup in both gloved hands. Chet had removed his right hand from his cup and lowered it to his right thigh. Yakima looked at Chet's right hand now, saw the index finger twitch.

Chet smiled grimly and glanced at the Yellowboy leaning against the log to Yakima's right. "How good are you with that Winchester, breed?"

"Good enough," Yakima said.

Tony narrowed one eye shrewdly as he said, "You're Yakima Henry, ain't you? Half-breed gunslinger..."

"Not really a gunslinger," Yakima said. "I pull iron when I have to. I don't go around lookin' for reasons." He paused, took another slow, casual sip of his coffee then slid his gaze between the two men before him. "You two ain't gonna give me a reason, now, are you?"

"Depends," Chet said.

"What do you want?" Tony said. "A share...?" He glanced at the saddlebags he'd laid out beside him. Both pouches had noticeable bulges. Both pouches of Chet's saddlebags did, too.

"Nope." Yakima slowly shook his head and crooked his mouth corners with a smile, his green eyes set deep in his copper-skinned face twinkling devilishly. "I want it all. And you."

"Us?" Tony asked, sliding a quick glance toward Chet.

"Bounty," Chet said, keeping his eyes on Yakima,

hardening his jaws and flaring a nostril. "They're offerin' a reward, ain't they? Back in Lone Pine."

"Two hundred for each of you...dead or alive," Yakima said.

"That ain't so much," Tony said.

"It's enough to stake me to a comfortable winter down in Mexico." Again, Yakima smiled. "Walkin' with some dusky-skinned senorita along the Sea of Cortez, the salty wind in our hair, a bottle of good tequila in my hand..."

"You got it all figured out," Chet said.

"He does, don't he?" Tony said, glancing at Chet again, the flush of anger now staining his cheeks. "He's got it all figured *out!*"

He dropped his coffee cup and grunted sharply as he thrust his right hand toward the walnut-butted Smith & Wesson holstered for the cross-draw on his left hip. Yakima dropped his own cup and felt the warm brew splash against his denims as he grabbed the Yellowboy, peeled the hammer back, aimed through the fire's dancing flames, and fired.

The Winchester barked sharply.

Tony screamed and flew straight back off his haunches, firing his Smith & Wesson over Yakima's right shoulder. Jerking the Yellowboy to his right as he cocked it, Yakima added a third roar to the echoes of the first two, his .44-caliber round punching through Chet's brisket, between the flaps of the robber's moisture-beaded rain slicker and hurling him straight back and down. Chet lay half in and half out of the cave, groaning, reaching again for the Colt Lightning that had not cleared leather the first time around.

Rising to his feet, Yakima shot him again and then hurled himself to his right as a gun flashed out in the rainy murk of the storm. He struck the cave floor as the rifle's thundering wail reached his ears. Cocking the Yellowboy once more, Yakima rolled back to his left, aimed the barrel around the fire, and sent three quick rounds screeching out into the storm.

He was rewarded with a bellowing wail and the sound of a body falling on the muddy downslope beyond the cave.

Chapter 2

"Just a kid," Yakima said.

He'd donned his rain slicker and stood gazing down now at the third outlaw who lay on his back at the bottom of the slope beneath the cave. This man was barely a man. He was somewhere in his late teens. He might have been twenty but no older than that. He had longish, flame-red hair. He was sharp featured, skinny, and long-limbed. A soot-stain mustache mantled his thin upper lip.

His hair had been splattered with mud, as had the rest of him, when he'd taken Yakima's bullet and rolled down the slope. Beneath his cream rain slicker, he wore denim trousers and a red-checked wool shirt and a red, neck-knotted bandana. A Colt revolver was thonged low on his skinny right thigh.

The muddy Winchester he'd fired into the cave lay a few feet away from him.

The kid, the guns, his rain slicker—everything was sodden and muddy.

Yakima cursed then leaned down and grabbed the kid's right arm. Crouching, he pulled the kid up over his shoulder and then started climbing the slope, slipping and falling on the muddy decline several times before, breathless and cursing, he reached the cave.

He laid the kid out beside the other two bank robbers, just outside the cave entrance. They no longer needed the benefit of the fire, and Yakima was revolted enough by death's specter to not want to share his overnight lodging with dead men.

He turned to look at Wolf. The black was staring at him with what he imagined was not so vague accusing.

"What're you lookin' at?" Yakima said, lifting his flat-brimmed, low-crowned black hat and running a hand through his long, wet, dark-brown hair. "How was I supposed to know the third owlhoot was a damn shaver?" He grunted and turned away, heading back down the slope, muttering to himself, "What was I supposed to do? *Not* punch his ticket? Let *him* punch *mine*?"

He found the robbers' two horses—a coyote dun and brown and white pinto—tied to a fir not far from where he'd found the kid at the base of the slope. He led both mounts up the slope, having to negotiate that muddy decline again in the pouring rain, then picketed them in some boulders away from Wolf, who was known to start fights with strange horses as a way of establishing dominance, which was likely the old Spanish stallion in him as well as a testament to his wild, mountain-bred roots.

He fed the mounts some parched corn from his own stores. There was water enough in the natural stone tanks around the horses, so Yakima didn't worry about filling his hat with rainwater, as he had for Wolf. He stripped the tack from both mounts then left them tied there in the boulders and returned, cold, wet, and shivering, his boots and the knees of his denims caked with mud, to the cave.

He removed his mud-streaked slicker and draped it lining-down over a flat rock just outside the cave.

Then he doffed his hat, squeezed the water out of his hair again, sat back down on his log, and poured himself a fresh cup of coffee to cut the chill that had seeped into his bones while he'd been toiling in the rain.

He hadn't been surprised the three bank robbers had found him. He'd figured they were holed up in these fir-stippled canyons between the San Juan and the Sawatch Range in south-central Colorado, awaiting a horse to replace the one they'd lost in Lone Pine when several gun-hung citizens had triggered lead at them, having taken it personally that their savings had just been plundered from the local Bank & Trust.

Yakima had learned of the robbery the following day

when he'd intended to stop in the town only long enough to replenish his trail supplies and to get a beer and maybe a woman if he saw one that fired his fancy. The posse the town marshal, who was an old army friend of Yakima, had organized had just returned—dusty, sweaty, weary, and frustrated. And with two of its members wrapped in their bedrolls riding belly down across their saddles.

Apparently, the catch party had caught up to the three robbers, two of whom were riding double, which had slowed down their getaway, and the posse had ridden into an ambush.

Word was going around Lone Pine that the president of the bank that had been robbed was offering a two-hundred-dollar reward for each of the three robbers, who'd robbed the bank while wearing flour sack masks, so their identities had been unknown. Now, Yakima was no bounty hunter. In fact, the breed revolted him.

But he'd ridden down from Dakota Territory with his pockets turned inside out and was looking for work. In Denver, he'd heard the Lone Pine area was producing some good color, so he'd decided to try his hand at prospecting, which he'd done in the past when he'd been sick to death of ranch work, bar tending, swamping out saloons or livery barns, and riding shotgun on stagecoaches. As a boy, he'd prospected in the Lone Pine area of Colorado Territory with his

German prospector father and his full-blood Cheyenne mother—not long before both had died, leaving him an orphan as a very young man.

Hunting the three bank-robbing killers had been an opportunity too good to pass up. While he was not a bounty hunter, he had hunted men before—men who'd needed hunting—and he'd proven right handy at it. And these three had definitely needed hunting. He wished he hadn't had to kill the kid, but he had, so there it was. If he could make a relatively quick six hundred dollars, he could continue riding south and into Mexico, staying ahead of the oncoming winter, and spend the next few months swilling tequila and frolicking with the senoritas.

Well, he'd made the six hundred dollars relatively quickly, but now he had that dead younker on his conscience. He'd killed many men before because he'd been forced to kill them. His had been a violent life, which the lives of most half-breeds on the wild western frontier usually were. Especially those that had found themselves uncommonly naturally good with a six-shooter and a throwing knife. Especially those who had for some reason thought it a good idea to allow a former Shaolin monk, whom Yakima had befriended while they'd both been laying railroad ties in the years after he'd mustered out of the frontier army, to fight using the sublime but deadly Eastern methods that included the use of hands as well as feet.

Thank God he'd never gotten to like killing—although he had become somewhat used to it—like some men did. But he didn't think he'd ever killed one as young as the kid lying glassy eyed in death out there in the rain, and the keys of his conscience were being strummed like those of an out of tune piano.

He didn't know why the kid's age mattered. A life was a life.

Still, it did. Maybe it had to do with the number of years he'd taken away.

He fished his whiskey bottle out of his saddlebags, sat down against the wooly underside of his saddle, added a liberal jigger of the unlabeled skull pop to his coffee, and sipped the coffee and whiskey and rolled and smoked a cigarette while gazing out into the rain, noting the gradual diminution of the storm before it petered out entirely and rolled northeast toward the Sawatch Range.

He remained there in the dripping silence, drinking, smoking, and brooding, feeling lonesome again as he always did as the night came down, longing for his dead wife Faith, former whore and the love of his life. The old saw was nevertheless poignant for being trite and sentimental—oh, what might have been had her former pimp, Bill Thornton, not killed her out of revenge for leaving him and lighting out to start a new life with the half-breed drifter, Yakima Henry...

What might have been.

A passel of kids. Life on the Arizona ranch they'd built side by side, often hand in hand. Many horses... birthdays and holidays celebrated. Then, after their allotment had been spent, children and grandchildren filling the house they'd left behind, the life they'd established, they would be two tombstones standing side-by-side in the Henry family plot there on the rocky, forested slopes of Mount Bailey.

Two kindred spirits having lived out their lives together now riding out eternity together.

Faith...

Yakima indulged his sorrow a good long time before, with the aid of the whiskey, which he switched solely to when he'd emptied the coffee pot, he allowed sleep to claim him.

Up early the next morning and still feeling foul, he built up the fire again and set coffee to boil. While the coffee cooked, Yakima grained and watered Wolf before saddling him then saddled the other two horses. He wrapped the bodies in the men's bedrolls and hoisted Roy and the kid over the beefiest of the two mounts, the coyote dun, and hoisted Chet over the slightly smaller brown-and-white calico. He lashed the legs and feet of the dead men together beneath the horses' bellies then returned to the cave to drink some coffee and eat some deer jerky.

As he did, he perused the sky over the canyon, glad to see a bright, clear Rocky Mountain day shaping up.

Should be a good day for travel. He hoped the flooding in the arroyos wouldn't impede him, for he wanted nothing more than to carry the three dead men back to Lone Pine, to claim the reward offered by the bank, and light a shuck south for Old Mexico and the dusky-eyed senoritas and the balmy, salty breezes blowing off the Sea of Cortez.

He closed his eyes and imagined the salt tang of that warm breeze in a girl's long, dark hair...

He washed a last bite of jerky down with his last sip of coffee, tossed the dregs on the fire, kicked out the flames, stowed his possibles in his saddlebags and warbag, grabbed his Yellowboy, and mounted up.

Leading the two pack horses by their bridle reins, Yakima put Wolf down the still-muddy hill and into the canyon then swung north, singing an old border song he remembered from long, desultory nights spent in the company of other men, some wielding guitars, in a mud-brick army barracks back at Camp Hell in Arizona, with a lemon rock candy moon kiting above the yucca and creosote brush, slanting spidery shadows across the rocky wastes beyond an open window shutter.

"What keeps the herd from running,

And stampede far and wide?
The cowboy's long, low whistle,
And singing by their side."

"Oh, it was a long and tiresome go,
Our herd rolled on to Mexico;
With music sweet of the cowboy song,
For Old Mexico we rolled along."

***

The afternoon of the next day, he rode into the bustling little ranch and mining supply town of Lone Pine, the giant shadow of the formidable Sawatch rising beyond it.

The town had been around awhile, and its longevity showed in the several brick as well as wood-frame, painted clapboard structures, including the large Cimarron Hotel. Of course, it wouldn't be a Colorado ranching and mining town if it didn't have a few impermanent wood-frame tent shacks, as well. One of these belonged to a faro dealer named Shawn O'Kelly and another to the Gypsy tarot card reader, Madame Cavalcanti, who stood outside her wood-framed tent now, on the main street's right side, smoking an opium pipe. She was a tall, slender Italian with an attractive, dark-eyed, oval-shaped face gaudied up with too much lipstick and rouge, her thick, black hair swept back under a purple turban trimmed with an ostrich feather.

Wearing a dress of dyed cotton that accentuated her curvaceous, high-busted figure, and Indian-beaded elk skin slippers, she leaned against her tent's doorframe, drawing on the long, slender pipe then exhaling slowly, dreamily. The cloying odor of the midnight oil reached Yakima's nose, and he pinched his hat brim to the woman whom, drunk, he'd visited the night he'd previously spent in Lone Pine. She'd seen much death in his past, but she'd assured him with a little too much nervous vigor that his chance at true love had not passed him by.

That buoyed him a little on the turbulent sea that was his life, even though he'd surmised that she probably told that to most of the men who visited her, drunk and owly at two in the morning, after spending an unsatisfactory couple of hours with a whore who knew all of the moves but had not been his lovely blue-eyed blond, Faith...

On a soft red cushion on a low table by the door of the woman's shack lounged a cat with jade eyes, long black fur, and a white-tipped tail. The cat blinked slowly at the passing rider atop the handsome black stallion, as did Madame Cavalcante, though her smile tightened when she took in the two packhorses, one carrying double, trotting along behind him.

He swung Wolf and the packhorses up to the town

marshal's humble log office just beyond Madame Cavalcante's and set a little back off the street. The pretty little
blond dressed in men's rustic trail garb including a snug
green plaid shirt said in a thick Southern accent over her
long, denim-clad legs and her scuffed boots crossed on
the porch rail before her, "Well, look what that gallblasted
cat has dragged in—*again!*"

She shaped a coquettish smile.

"Hi, Yakima."

Chapter 3

"Hi, Pearl."

Pearl O'Malley dropped her feet to the floor as she slid her gaze back to the two horses sitting behind Yakima and Wolf. "You ran 'em down, didn't you?" She rose from her chair, eyes wide and eager. "Already, you ran 'em down! Pa said you would! He said you were the best Injun fighter at the—"

"Where is your pa?" Yakima interrupted her. Pearl's father was the Lone Pine Town Marshal, George O'Malley. An old friend of his.

Yakima had known O'Malley in the army, when they'd both been stationed at Fort Hildebrandt, otherwise known as "Camp Hell," fighting the Apaches together, Yakima as a civilian scout and tracker. He'd gotten reacquainted with O'Malley, who'd been a sergeant at Hildebrandt, when Yakima had ridden through town the other day after the robbery and had spied the stout, portly, red-faced, familiar looking old Irishman sporting a five-pointed silver star. O'Malley had been sitting out here, where Pearl was now standing, regarding the three dead men lying belly down across the two horses' backs. A bum hip had kept O'Malley from riding out with the posse he'd sent after the bank robbers.

Pearl had been cleaning her father's office at the time, and O'Malley had introduced his nineteen-year-old daughter to Yakima, punctuating the introduction with a warning look that told Yakima in no uncertain terms that the pretty blonde with the sparkling blue eyes and fetching Southern accent was off-limits. Inwardly, Yakima had chuckled at that.

Even back at Fort Hell, when he'd been tracking Apaches with his partner, Seth Barksdale, Yakima's reputation for having an eye for the ladies had preceded him. O'Malley needn't have worried, however. Having gotten whipsawed between two beautiful sisters in Apache Springs, a bustling little railroad and mining town in Arizona Territory's Chiricahua Mountains, Yakima was staying away from all females of the non-professional variety. Whores were a lot less trouble than regular women, and Pearl O'Malley, with the way she filled out her man's wool shirt, pulled back against her breasts by her suspenders, and that wild glint in her large blue eyes, had trouble with a capital 'T' written all over her...

"Pa's inside," Pearl said, jerking her head back to indicate the marshal's humble office behind her. "Sufferin' from the flue, don't ya know—of the bottle variety." She lifted her extended right thumb to her mouth and jerked her head back again, this time taking an imaginary drink of her father's beloved skull pop.

While Yakima's reputation for having an eye for the ladies may have preceded *him*, the former Sergeant George O'Malley's reputation for having the traditional Irishman's fondness for the who-hit-John preceded *him*.

"I heard that!" came a deep, gravelly voice from inside the marshal's office. "Yakima back?"

"He sure is, Pa!" Pearl hurried down the porch's three steps and into the street. "He took 'em down, Pa, just like you said he would! Hey, get away from there, you urchins. Were you raised by *wolves*? Get away. *Git!*" Pearl said, addressing the three little boys—two tow-heads and an even smaller, brown-headed youngster in homespun bibbed overalls who'd skulked up to inspect the two dead men lying sprawled across the brown-and-white pinto.

Turning now to regard the youngsters, who were accompanied by a short-haired yellow dog, Yakima saw that he'd attracted a small crowd of on-lookers who'd gathered on both sides of the street, muttering among themselves.

A bearded man in a bullet-crowned black hat standing with two others on the boardwalk fronting a tonsorial parlor yelled to the boys, "Is that who I think it is, Kenny?"

One of the two tow-heads, Kenny, ignored Pearl's orders and squatted down beside the pinto and parted the blanket in which Yakima had wrapped the young man he'd killed the previous night, exposing the face. The kid's long, red hair had slipped out from a fold in the blanket. Kenny turned his flushed face toward the man who'd spoken and said, "Sure is, Pa! It's him, all right! It's Weldon Stratton!"

"Get away from there, Kenny, or I'll tan your rotten little hide!" Pearl said, giving Kenny's skinny rump a kick with the side of her boot as he ran off with the other two boys and the barking dog.

"Go easy on my boy, Pearl!" yelled the man in the bullet-crowned hat, pointing an admonishing finger at the pretty young blond. "The only one who tan's Kenny's hide is me!"

"Yeah, well, you oughta do it a little more often, Pee-bles!" Pearl shot back. "That kid's gonna grow up to be a regular guest at Pa's jail!"

Pearl turned to look down at the young man lying belly down across the pinto. She looked up at Yakima still sitting his saddle. She had a grave, worried look in her pretty blue eyes now. She moved her lips, tentatively,

30

as though to speak but apparently thought better of it. Saying nothing, she crouched low to part the blankets, revealing the face of the dead young man.

"Who's Weldon Stratton?" Yakima asked her, hipped around in his saddle, his right, gloved hand resting on the bedroll behind him.

"*Who?*" This from the porch of the marshal's office, where George O'Malley, whose nickname at Fort Hell had been "Sarge," now stood just outside the open door, scowling curiously between Yakima and his uneasy-looking daughter. He was a big, broad-shouldered, heavy-gutted man with a head of thinning, curly, salt-and-pepper hair. He had the traditional red nose of a heavy drinker.

"Weldon Stratton," Yakima said. "Who is—?"

"You better come over an' see this, Pa," Pearl interrupted him.

"Is it him?" asked her father.

Pearl drew a deep breath and, on the exhale, said, "Yep."

A gasp rose from somewhere behind Yakima. He heard it beneath the growing hum of the men and even a few women, mostly of the painted variety, gathered on the boardwalks on both sides of the street.

"*Who?*" A woman's voice joined the chorus of disbelief.

Yakima turned to see a pretty, brown-eyed, olive-skinned woman, probably in her late thirties and clad in a fancy but conservatively cut burnt-orange gown and waistcoat over a ruffled white silk blouse, move toward Pearl and the pinto, hiking the skirt of her gown above her high-heeled, side-button shoes. She was moving straight out away from the Bank & Trust in front of which several men in three-piece suits were also gathered, conversing in hushed tones.

Pearl turned to the woman, then, as well, and her expression turned a shade darker than before. She said nothing but took one halting step back away from the dead young man, whose blanketed torso hung down over the pinto's right side. The woman slowed as she approached the dead younker and then slowly bent her knees, squatting and tilting her head so she could view the dead boy's face peeking out from the opened fold in the blankets.

As she did, her lips parted. Her mouth opened slowly, and her brown eyes widened in shock.

Just as quickly as her shock had shone itself on her pretty, olive-skinned, heart-shaped face, her expression grew sorrowful. She narrowed her eyes, shallow lines spoking out from their corners and deeper lines cutting across her forehead. She reached up with her right hand and placed it against the side of the dead boy's face, staring at the kid through those narrowed eyes that Yakima thought for sure were about to rain real tears.

He sat there, that bayonet of guilt really plundering his guts now.

George O'Malley came down off the porch, adjusting the suspenders holding his baggy, wash-faded denims up on his broad hips, and walked toward the pinto, his own expression one of great sadness. "I'm...I'm sorry, Beatriz," he said, haltingly.

Yakima gave a deep sigh as he swung down from his saddle to walk over and stand near where the dusky-eyed woman still knelt beside the dead boy, placing her hand against the side of his cold, pale cheek.

"Who is he?" Yakima asked, addressing his question to no one in particular but to Pearl, O'Malley, and the pretty brunette in general. His heart thudded heavily, and he felt sick to his stomach, as though he'd just chugged a crock of sour milk.

Someone's son. This woman's son? He saw no family resemblance. She appeared to have some Spanish blood. The dead kid was skinny yet raw-boned and fair-skinned, with that flame-red hair.

"Come on," he pleaded, his voice pitched low with his own brand of sadness now. "I gotta know. Who'd I kill?"

The murmuring issuing from both sides of the street gradually grew louder as more and more people joined the crowds milling on boardwalks on both sides of the street. All eyes were on the woman crouching over the dead boy, holding her slender hand against his cheek with great affection.

"You didn't kill him, Mister Henry," she said now, her eyes on the boy.

She removed her hand from the boy's face and rose. She kept her eyes on the boy for another few seconds and then turned to Yakima, her rich, deep-brown, almond-shaped eyes cast with unassuageable grief though they were still dry. She pressed her right hand against her bosom, and said, "I did."

She turned and walked back in the direction of the bank, all eyes on her now, a sudden quiet having fallen over the street.

Suddenly, as though having forgotten something, she stopped and turned back to Yakima. "Follow me," she said in her formal, Spanish-accented voice. "We will settle up inside."

She turned again and continued walking toward the bank. Yakima watched her step up onto the boardwalk, the several men gathered there quickly making way for her. She pushed through the bank's heavy door, the bell over the door ringing, the door's upper, curtained window glinting in the afternoon sun.

Then she was gone.

Yakima turned to George O'Malley standing beside him.

"Who is she, Sarge?"

"Beatriz Salazar." The marshal shared a meaningful look with Pearl then drew a deep breath, filling up his lumpy chest, and said, "She's the banker who issued the reward on them three's heads," he added, glancing down at the three dead men. The two dead men and the boy, rather. "And now there's gonna be holy hell to pay."

He whistled softly, glancing at Pearl and shaking his head.

"How so?" Yakima said, growing deeply annoyed at the amount of information he was being deprived of.

"Let her tell it," Pearl said, lifting her chin to indicate the bank.

The marshal set his big hand on Yakima's shoulder. "Go on in and get your pay. Don't worry about it. It ain't your fault, Yakima. If you shot him, you had to shoot him. I know that. They shot two posse riders. You earned your money. Now, go get it and I'll buy you a beer. Hell, I'll buy you two beers, a whiskey and a steak. You look like you could use every bit of it. And now, so could I," the big man added, casting his dark gaze to the bank. "Go ahead. I'll send for the undertaker and cut them bodies down from the horses."

Yakima cursed in frustration then walked over to his horse, grabbed the swollen pair of saddlebags off of Wolf's back, and draped them over his left shoulder, leaving his right hand free for his gun. He habitually left his right hand free for his gun but now he did it as a conscious precaution, for he felt as though every eye in town was on him, silently condemning him for killing the kid though no one could have condemned him any more than he condemned himself—especially after seeing the look on the face of the woman who'd placed the bounty on the kid's head.

He swung around and tramped toward the bank. The same men who'd made way for the woman made way for him now, looking him up and down, appearing impressed by his size as well as the exoticness of his jade-eyed, copper-skinned appearance, long, dark-brown hair tumbling down from his flat-crowned black hat. They looked at the horn-gripped Colt .44 thonged low on his right thigh, as well.

Gunfighter-style.

Yeah, they were impressed by his appearance. Wary, too. A big half-breed who wore a gun like he knew how to use it. An Arkansas toothpick sheathed on his left hip. Nothing more dangerous than a big, well-armed half-breed. One who'd taken down three men all by himself.

Yakima stepped into the bank, the bell rattling over the door. He squinted, his eyes adjusting to the bank's deep shadows, probing the place. There appeared no customers. Two tellers gazed out at him from two of the three cages to his left. Three men sat behind a low, wooden rail, at heavy wooden desks trimmed with green-shaded Tiffany lamps to his right. All three wore suits, celluloid collars, neckties, and stylish mustaches or carefully trimmed beards. Their hair was carefully combed. The air smelled of pomade.

All three bankers stared at him from the shadows of their respective desks flanked by filing cabinets and bookshelves, slowly blinking their eyes. The information about who he was and what he'd done had obviously made its way into the bank. Yakima could see it in the cautious eyes clinging to him like a fish on a hook, unable to let it go.

A big half-breed in dusty trail clothes in a bank. How often did you see that? Yakima rarely saw the inside of a bank. He so rarely had opportunity to. On the rare occasion that he had, he knew the rest of the clientele and banking associates were thinking he was there to rob the place...

One of the men—pale and bespectacled and wearing a green eyeshade—glanced at the partly open door in the wall across the lobby from Yakima, and said, "Miss Salazar is in there..." He tilted his soft, beringed, right hand, indicating the door.

Yakima strode toward it, the heels of his boots clacking on the varnished wooden floor puncheons. A gold nameplate on the door read: BEATRIZ SALAZAR, PRESIDENT.

Hmm, Yakima thought. *A lady bank president.*

He'd known few of those. No, he'd never known a lady bank president. Now, however, it appeared he was going to know this one though he'd be damned if, under the circumstances, he wanted to. He did want a few answers, though. Namely, who in the hell was the boy he'd killed and what in holy blazes was the kid doing robbing her bank if she'd felt such great affection for him?

Removing his hat, Yakima nudged the door wide and stopped just inside. She sat at a big desk before him, crouched over what appeared a large, leathered-covered, open book of bank drafts. She was scratching on one of the blanks with a nib pen.

"I don't want your money, lady." Yakima walked up and dropped the saddlebags on one of the two, red-upholstered guest chairs positioned before the desk, facing it. "Not for killing no kid. Especially one you seem to have a great deal of feeling for. Who was he?"

She lifted the pen from the check blank and looked up at him, her Spanish-dark eyes reflecting the light from the windows behind him. "No one to you," she said matter-of-factly, almost coldly. "You held up your end of the bargain. Now I will hold up mine."

She turned and lowered her head and resumed

scribbling on the blank. She tore the draft from the book and held it out to him.

When he didn't take it, but stood looming over her, staring implacably down at her, she sat back in her chair and studied him skeptically. She turned her head slightly to one side and narrowed one eye at him. "What? A killer with a heart?"

"Never mind," Yakima said, anger flaring in him.

He turned and strode back to the door, leaving her with the check blank drooping from her long, slender right hand.

"I'll get my answers elsewhere."

He walked across the lobby and out of the bank.

Chapter 4

"Spill it, Sarge," he told O'Malley later, when they'd sat down together in the Rawhider Saloon, each with a beer and a shot of whiskey on the table before them. Yakima hadn't touched either drink yet. He had more important things on his mind. "Who was the kid? Who was he to *her*?"

O'Malley scowled down at his dimpled schooner and frowned pensively as he stuck a sausage-like finger into the foam and stirred it. He licked the foam off his finger and then scowled across the table at Yakima. "The son of a friend of hers. The son of an old friend of hers. Let's just leave it at that."

Yakima frowned back at the man. "What kind of friend raises a son to rob your bank then shoot two posse riders?"

"Their, uh…relationship—well, it's complicated."

O'Malley looked around the bustling saloon as though to make sure none of the miners and range men patronizing the place—a rowdy, unwashed lot, some with painted ladies on their knees—was leaning in, eavesdropping on his and Yakima's conversation.

He continued with: "No one talks about it anymore. Everyone knows, but no one talks about it...lest they should get a bullet in the back or a knife across the throat. Sort of a town-wide—hell, *county*-wide—agreement. I'd just as soon not go into it, either. That's all you need to know. The son of an old friend. Now, take my advice and ride out of town first thing in the morning."

Yakima sat staring at his old friend, his arms on the table, sort of hooked around the whiskey shot and the beer, both of which he still hadn't sampled. Slowly, stubbornly, he shook his head. "I'm staying right here in Lone Pine until I get the full story about who I killed an' why I had to kill him."

O'Malley looked back at him and grimaced. "Oh, hell, Yakima!"

He picked up his shot glass between his right thumb and index finger and threw back the entire shot in one fell swoop. He slammed the glass back down on the table, scrubbed a grimy shirtsleeve across his mustached mouth, then looked around the room again, cautiously.

At the nearest table, a young doxie who couldn't have been much older than the kid Yakima had killed sat on the lap of a bib-bearded gent, likely a miner, and was laughing and pulling his ears. She had nothing on from the waist up except a couple of strands of fake pearls. While she played with his ears, the miner played with her wares, his eyes bright with drink and carnal merriment. They had no interest in Yakima and the Lone Pine marshal's conversation.

O'Malley turned back to Yakima. "All right—here it is. But keep this under your hat, understand?"

Yakima assured him he would.

O'Malley leaned over his beer, shoving his big, raw-boned face up to Yakima and said, "Back when they was kids—little girls—Beatriz Salazar and Renee Stratton was best friends. This was when Lone Pine was a third of the size it is now, and Beatriz's father came up here from New Mexico, after the girl's mother died. Diego Salazar is dead now, been dead several years. Beatriz has been working in the bank since she was knee high to a jackrabbit, so she took it over from Diego. She's been runnin' it ever since he died."

"Fer chrissakes, Sarge—get to the kid!"

"Look, if you wanna understand the situation, you have to hear the whole story!"

Yakima sighed, shook his head, and threw back half of his whiskey to calm his nerves.

"Renee Stratton is a rich rancher's daughter. Lives up on the bench where there's good grass. She and Beatriz were once best friends. Their fathers were business partners, you see? Beatriz spent time out at the Stratton Ranch—the Bear Track—and Renee would spend equal time here in town with Beatriz. When a school opened, they went to school together. That's where they both met a boy named Daniel Stockbridge."

Again, O'Malley took a quick look around then lifted his schooner and took a couple of deep swallows of the frothy ale. He set the glass back down, drew a breath as though to calm himself, and continued with, "Beatriz, Renee, and Daniel palled around together for several years, until they were around nineteen or so. Then Renee and Daniel sort of paired off, and suddenly Beatriz was out of the picture."

"Hmmm..." Yakima said, slowly nodding. The story was getting more interesting though something told him in a dark sort of way...

"Renee and Daniel married. Big wedding. The elder Weldon Stratton never did anything small. A big church weddin' and a town-wide celebration! That was damn near twenty years ago." O'Malley shook his head as he stared down at his beer. "How time does fly!"

"The kid was theirs?" Yakima prodded the big man. "Renee an' Daniel's?"

O'Malley kept his eyes on his beer, as though the foam crackling on top of it were a frosted window looking into the past. "That's right. He came only a few months after the wedding. It was a scandal for a time, but a small one, the players being who they were—powerful people in this county. The Bear Track is a big, formidable outfit." He smiled ruefully. "A little bit outlaw. Folks talked about it to their own peril. Everyone was afraid of Weldon Stratton...just like they're now afraid of his daughter, Renee."

The big marshal shook his head as though to get himself back on track. "Anyway, the boy—named Weldon after Renee's father—was a little simple." He tapped his temple. "And hard to handle. A bully to other kids. Was *unkind* to animals, I hear," he added with a caustic chuff. "Still, Renee loved him dearly. Word has it, Daniel didn't feel as strongly about the boy as she did, and that caused a rift in their marriage. Starting a few years back, you rarely saw Renee and Daniel together in town anymore. Now when Renee drove a wagon into town for supplies, it was always just with Weldon."

Yakima nodded, frowning curiously.

"Here's where it gets complicated," the lawman said, lifting his grave gaze to Yakima now.

He took another quick look around. The doxie and the miner had gone upstairs, so that table was now vacant. That seemed to set O'Malley at ease.

He took another pull from his beer and, keeping his voice low and leaning forward over the table, said, "About three years ago, there was trouble. Big trouble."

Yakima waited.

"Renee was out picking berries for pie one summer afternoon. Beatriz was going to drive out for pie and coffee with Renee and Daniel. When she rode back to the main house there at the Bear Track, she went inside to find Beatriz and Daniel in bed together."

Yakima whistled his surprise.

"Renee went into a rage," O'Malley said. "She found a gun and was about to shoot Beatriz, but Daniel stepped between them. He took the bullet in his guts. Took him several days to die."

"Jesus!" Yakima said.

The story had definitely taken a dark turn, all right.

O'Malley sat staring down into his beer, slowly shaking his head.

"What happened next, Sarge?" Yakima prodded him.

O'Malley winced as he tugged absently on his mustache.

He shrugged and said, "Nothing much. The whole thing...well, we covered it up. Me, the local prosecutor... Weldon Stratton." His mouth had twisted a look of bitter distaste and self-deprecation. "You know—powerful people. We called it a case of mistaken identity. Renee mistook her husband for an intruder and, frightened out of her wits, shot him. Beatriz wasn't there, of course."

"Beatriz went along with the story, too, I take it?"

"She felt as responsible as Renee did. I'm told they both mourned equally except now one hates the other and the other lives under a big, dark cloud of guilt and heartbreak. I don't think I've ever seen Beatriz without sadness in her eyes. Not since that day Daniel died.

"Likely, the whole thing would have been swept under the rug out there at the Bear Track. No one would have known what really happened. Except the two parties didn't trust each other—Renee and her father and Beatriz. So old Weldon came to my office and we summoned the county sheriff an' the judge and the district prosecutor, an' did the dirty deed right then and there. Covered the whole thing up. Made the lie official, stamped and filed it."

Yakima sipped his beer. "I see now why Beatriz's reaction to the kid's death was complicated. Her old friend's son. Her lover's son. Her lover who died because of her. The way she probably sees it, anyways."

"Yep, Weldon the younger was the son of Beatriz's former best friend. Only that best friend is now her blood enemy." O'Malley chuckled without mirth. "Yeah, it's complicated."

"Jesus."

"Yeah."

"Keep going, Sarge." There had to be more.

Again, O'Malley tapped his temple. "I heard around

a year ago that Renee kind of cracked her nut, if you know what I mean. Drunk as she often is these days, she was overheard vowing to someone over at the Cimarron Hotel, where she keeps a suite of rooms, that someday she was going to make Beatriz suffer for her sins. And suffer in *grand fashion*. That there is a direct quote."

Yakima glowered skeptically. "You think she sent her son to rob Beatriz's bank?"

O'Malley shook his head. "For years, she's been trying to keep Weldon *out* of trouble. I don't think Renee had anything to do with the robbery. That was Weldon himself. You can bet the seed bull he knew how his ma felt about Beatriz. He started runnin' with them other two raggedy-heeled wannabe outlaws, Chet Fitzgerald and Roy Wannamaker, about a year ago. Apparently, his mother couldn't control him no longer. I hear she drinks most of the day, Renee does. Moons around in that big house all by herself..."

Yakima finished off his whiskey and washed it down with a couple of deep pulls from his mug. After hearing all that...after learning the whipsaw he'd wandered into out here when he'd just been trying to make some traveling cash...he needed every drop of the who-hit-John he could get. He had to keep his wolf on its leash, though. He knew all too well what happened when he didn't, when he dove too deep into the bottle.

It wasn't good. It usually involved a ruined saloon and jail time.

He ran his sleeve across his mouth and looked fatefully across the table at his old friend. "You think this'll set her off, don't you? Renee. Send her after Beatriz."

"I don't know. Hard to say. I don't know how she is anymore. Used to see her in town a lot. She'd have dinner at the hotel. Now I hear she mostly just stays up at the ranch, in her cups most of the time. Anyway, it ain't your worry, Yakima. You killed the kid in self-defense. I know it wouldn't have happened any other way. You just light on out of here tomorrow, at first light. It ain't your problem. I'll keep a close eye on Beatriz."

"I killed that kid, Sarge. If Renee goes after anyone, she should come after me. If I'm not here, she might go after Beatriz. I already have blood on my hands. I don't want her blood on my hands now, too."

O'Malley drew a deep breath and shook his head. "Yakima, dammit, you're only gonna make things worse."

"How? By deflecting attention from Beatriz?"

O'Malley pointed an accusing finger at Yakima. "I know you. If you stay here, you'll detonate a powder keg. So, she sends men after you. You go after her. That's nothin' but trouble an' I got enough trouble in this town without you addin' to it. No, we haven't seen each other in fifteen years, but your reputation precedes you, Yakima!"

"They exaggerate."

"Yeah, well I got a federal wanted circular in my office that don't sound like an exaggeration to me. And it's current."

"Ah, hell!"

"Yeah."

"You'd sic the federals on me? Them two deputy U.S. marshals I killed were ridin' the wrong side of the law." It was true. The two federals Yakima had killed had been siding with cattle rustlers in southern Arizona. Yakima had been on the side of the smaller Mexican ranchers who'd been ranching in the area a whole lot longer than the whites had. Besides, one of the lawmen had been about to rape a senorita.

As true as it was, he had federal paper on his head. Federal paper didn't go away. That federal paper was keeping him from settling down and living the peaceful life he so desired.

O'Malley polished off his beer and rose heavily from his chair. "You an' me go back, Yakima. An' that's worth somethin'. But it's not worth letting you start a war, which I know you'd do if you stayed around here, parrying blows with Renee Stratton. You ride out tomorrow at first light, or I'll walk over to the telegraph office."

Yakima just glowered up at the man, his belly a knot of frustration. He wasn't the kind of man who didn't tie up his own loose ends, but it looked as though that was what he was being forced to do here.

Suddenly, O'Malley grinned and shoved a big, meaty paw over the table at him. "Still friends?"

Yakima grunted. "What the hell?" he drawled. "I reckon I got few enough I can't afford to lose one I have." He shook the man's hand.

"Go to bed early, Yakima." O'Malley headed for the door.

PETER BRANDVOLD

Chapter 5

It was a lead pipe cinch Garth McCowan was going to kill his horse if he didn't slow it down. But he couldn't do it. He had to get back to the Bear Track as fast as the dun could run. He wanted—no, he *had to be*—the one to deliver the news to his boss of what he'd learned in town.

He had to be the one so he could defuse her. Because, if there was one thing he knew about his boss, Renee Stratton, it was that as soon as she found out that her son was dead and who'd paid the bounty on his head, all hell was going to pop. McGowan had managed to restrain her so far on the subject of her old friend, Beatriz Salazar, over these past three years. It would truly be a shame if all that effort and restraint went to hell now and she burned the whole damn place to the ground.

Especially since the world, frankly, was a better place without that useless firebrand, young Weldon, in it...

Riding hunkered low over his horse's long neck, Mc-Gowan, foreman of the Bear Track—a rangy, broad-shouldered, and muscular man even now in his late forties though growing a bulge around his middle—chuffed a caustic snort and gave his head a single, fateful wag.

"Come on, Rebel, dammit," McGowan urged the dun, slapping his rein ends against the galloping horse's right hip. "Don't slow on me now, boy! Just one more mile... just over that next rise...and we're home!"

Home.

Yeah, that's what the Bear Track was. That's what the Bear Track *had been* to him for the past twenty damn years, since the old man himself, Weldon Stratton, had hired him after he'd moved his herd up here after a bitter range war in west Texas...and with a bounty on the old man's head. Stratton had been only 49 at the time, but McGowan had always seen Weldon Stratton as the Old Man. A grand old red-faced, raging lion even at 49, and the old bastard went out raging at age 76, not long after the, um, *incident* that had claimed the life of the man he'd hoped would shepherd his ranch into the next century—Daniel Stockbridge, who'd turned out be a surprisingly effective range manager despite having been a town kid.

Weldon Stratton, the elder, had had no sons of his own. Renee had been his first-born, and when she'd come into this world, raging not unlike her father when he'd left it, she'd taken away his opportunity for having any sons in the future. She'd come out so violently that she'd killed her mother in a literal blood bath. She'd left the poor woman, the dear, sweet Ruthie who'd deserved a much better end for having to live with the tyrant she'd married, gasping and choking and strangling on her own blood.

She and the old man were gone now.

Now, only Renee and the boy lived in the big old lodge, though the boy had rarely been around for the past several years, after he'd turned sixteen and for some reason decided that that was a good age for unleashing his wolf once and for all and for good. The little viper had taken after his grandfather that way. But in that way only. The younger Weldon had been soft in his thinker box, whereas his grandfather had been damn near the smartest man Garth McGowan had ever known. That's what had made him such a damned good rancher, and so damned cunning and dangerous

Yeah, the place had been McGowan's home for the past twenty years. He was counting on it being his home for the next twenty, thirty—for however long the rest of his allotment turned out to be. He deserved to remain here. He'd helped build this place, by God. And he, often single-handedly, kept it running, kept it producing, kept it from being overrun by miners and nesters and rustlers and rival ranchers who'd love nothing more than to claim the Bear Track range for their own.

The fact of the matter was McGowan had nowhere else to go.

And he wasn't getting any younger. He didn't want to find himself without a roof over his head and steady wages, because it was not easy for a man his age to find work. Even if another rancher would hire him, at his age, he didn't want to have to start fresh on some foreign spread, working for a man...a family...other hands...he wasn't familiar with.

The Bear Track was his home and he wanted to keep it that, but the only way he could keep it that was if he could keep the high-strung Bear Track mistress from destroying it. From destroying herself and the ranch and McGowan, to boot.

From burning her life and Garth's life all the way to the damn ground.

McGowan had gotten word an hour ago about the kid's death. He'd been riding into Lone Pine from the eastern range and noted the commotion on the street. An old former cowhand, Henry Waddell, had come over from the porch of one of the saloons and told him the news. He'd explained the whole story—the bounty, the half-breed bounty Hunter, and dead Weldon being hauled back to town tied over the saddle of his horse.

Now, McGowan was afraid another rider had ridden out ahead of him to relay the news to his boss. Renee had fawning servants everywhere because, like her friend Beatriz Salazar, though she was pushing forty, she still looked a good ten years younger.

Raving damned beauties even in their late thirties, both women.

A beauty that in Renee's case masked the heart of a lion, restless and fiery even in repose...

Why in the hell had Beatriz gone and slept with McGowan's boss, Daniel Stockbridge? That incident three years ago had been the start of McGowan's deep, bone-rattling anxiousness and long, sleepless nights, wondering how to keep his boss on her leash without her realizing he was keeping her on her leash. If she ever realized he was trying to control her, that would be the end of his control.

"What the hell you doin', Garth? You tryin' to kill that hoss!" scolded the Bear Track's senior hostler, Roy "Pops" Eberhart as McGowan reined in the wobbly-legged dun in the middle of the ranch yard.

The bandy-legged oldster was coming out of the barn, scowling as he took in the blown, sweat-lathered dun.

"I had no choice, Pops," McGowan complained, swinging his right leg over the saddle horn and dropping straight down to the ground. Turning to face the old, leathery-faced, gaunt-cheeked hostler who'd just grabbed the horse's cheek strap, he said, "The boss is in, isn't she?"

"Does she ever go *anywhere?*"

"Has anybody else been here? Within the past hour?"

Eberhart shook his head. "Nope. All quiet." He hooked a thumb to indicate the lone cowboy walking a gray pony around the breaking corral by its halter rope. "Chance and I are the only ones here. The other hands are still shifting the herds around like you told 'em this morning."

He turned to regard the blowing dun once more then returned his incredulous gaze to the big, red-faced, brown-haired and mustached foreman who'd just swung around to walk over to the big log house on the opposite side of the yard from the barn. "What the hell's gotten into you, Garth?"

"Later, Pops," the foreman said with a quick, parting wave.

He removed his hat and swatted the dust from it against his thighs as he tramped toward the big lodge that the old man had built with the help of McGowan himself and a dozen of the first hands ever hired on the place. It was a grand lodge by anyone's standards—a massive, three-story, log barrack with a wide verandah on three sides and large windows in every wall so that the old man needn't bother to turn his leonine head to look out and admire his holdings—ten thousand acres of prime San

Juan Valley graze that he and McGowan and the other hands had fought away from the Indians.

Back in those days, they'd scalped the savages and hung the trophies on the bunkhouse wall.

Now he climbed the broad, front, halve-logged steps and crossed the veranda, stomping the dust from his boots on the hemp matt in front of it. He pounded on the door three times with his fist, loudly, for it was a big house and she could be anywhere. He didn't wait for her reply but opened the heavy door and stepped inside, stopping suddenly.

She must have been in the kitchen because she stood now in the doorway that let into the kitchen, just ahead and to McGowan's left. She held a drink in her hand as she usually did this time of the day—which was to say anytime after noon. She must have been cooking, though, because she wore an apron. She looked strange in an apron, probably because he couldn't recollect ever seeing her in one. She and the old man had always hired cooks, but she'd fired the last one and, given her reputation, was having trouble finding another.

She aimed a spatula at him and narrowed one of her striking gray eyes that off-set the fire-red of her hair to beautiful affect, even when she was stewed. "You kill one of my horses and I'm taking it out of your pay as well as your hide, Garth!"

"Sorry, boss." Even though they'd slept together, he still called her "boss." Out of long habit, he had trouble addressing her by her first name. "Couldn't be helped. I, uh"—he doffed his hat—"can I come in?"

She crooked a lusty smile, spreading her broad, red lips. She was a small, supple woman, but she radiated great strength and self-possession. Her curly red hair, which hung down well past her shoulders and was still without a strand of gray, shone in the light angling through the still-open door. It sparkled in her eyes. Her simple vanilla-colored day dress was cut low, showing a good bit of creamy, freckled cleavage. Proud of her body, she liked to show it off, and having lived amongst men her entire life, she'd had ample opportunity for which she'd been duly rewarded in the reactions she'd invited.

She was an image out of a Celtic warrior's dream. Always had been. Always would be. No matter how much she drank.

"You didn't blow out that horse just for me, did you, Garth?" she asked now, lowering the spatula and leaning against the doorframe, the bodice of the dress rising as her breasts swelled.

McGowan felt his cheeks warm. She was the only woman who could still make him blush.

He stepped forward, took her arm in his hand. "Let's walk into the study. We need to discuss something..."

Discuss something. Right…

When she'd found out what had happened to that devil spawn of hers, there would be no discussion.

When she resisted the light tug of his hand, he glanced back at her. She frowned up at him curiously, maybe even a little apprehensively. She said nothing.

"Come on, boss. Let's freshen that drink of yours. Maybe I'll even have one."

"I'm cooking." She smiled again, that amorous glint returning to her eyes. "Maybe I'll cook for you tonight, Garth."

It was his turn to frown. "You never cook for me. Remember, you said you'd never cook for me because you didn't want me to see you that way." She let him keep a room in the house but on her own terms. When she'd finished with him in her room, he didn't linger. No soft, sensual kisses and cuddling under the sheets afterwards. No, when she'd taken her satisfaction, he slipped out of bed and returned to his own room. She hadn't had to tell him. He just knew.

But he'd be damned if he didn't look forward to being summoned again with a simple sidelong glance with those intoxicating gray eyes. She was the only woman who could make him blush. The only woman who could treat him like so much horse flesh, and he'd keep coming back for more.

"Maybe I've changed my mind," she said, caressing the door frame through that tight frock with her hip.

"Not tonight." McGowan gave her a more insistent tug with his hand. "Come on, boss. Let's have a drink...a chat."

A chat.

Right.

Chapter 6

McGowan led Renee into her father's study stuffed practically to the ceiling beams with dusty books on range management, bovine and equestrian medicine, as well as big, heavy tomes that betrayed old Weldon's improbable love for classical literature. No one who had ever known the old lion would have suspected he'd loved literature. McGowan suspected that the only two people alive who did know were himself and Renee, who did not share her father's passion for reading.

The study remained as the old man had left it—dusty and cluttered, overstuffed with masculine wood and leather furniture including a large mahogany, hide-covered desk, and rife with the smell of the old man's pipes and cigars and his favorite Kentucky bourbon as well as smoke from the now-cold brick hearth.

Aware of Renee's puzzled scrutiny, the foreman retrieved the heavy, green, cut-glass bourbon decanter from the liquor cabinet, took it over to where she slumped in a cracked leather armchair that dwarfed her, and replenished the whiskey in her nearly empty glass. Her cat-like eyes were glued to his, the freckled skin above the bridge of her nose wrinkled with speculation and curiosity.

McGowan returned the decanter to the liquor cabinet. He walked back over to where Renee sat by the hearth and sank into a leather chair that matched her own and that faced hers from the other side of a low, cherry coffee table strewn with account books, file folders, old newspapers, pencil stubs and their shavings, loose business documents and scribbled notes, some coffee-stained and scorched with ancient cigar ash, yellowing with age.

"Where's your drink?"

"What?" he said.

She glanced at his empty hands. "You're not drinking."

"I'm going to stay clear."

Renee gave a crooked smile, shook her head, and said softly but with insistence, "Drink with me, Garth."

He stared back at her as he leaned forward, his elbows on his knees.

That crooked smile remaining on her full mouth, she slid her eyes toward the liquor cabinet, a subtle command.

The foreman rose with a sigh.

He walked over to the liquor cabinet, pulled a goblet

off the dusty pyramid, and splashed a couple of jiggers of bourbon into it. He stood there at the cabinet, facing a window that had a thin, cream, see-through curtain drawn over it. The heavy umber drapes were pulled back to offer a view of the Ponderosa-stippled hillside rising behind the house.

On that hillside, an old wooden wheelbarrow was turned upside down against a large rock. McGowan remembered the old man using the wheelbarrow to garden in the spring, pushing dirt and transplanted shrubs around. He often pushed his grandson around in that wheelbarrow, as well, the little boy goo-gawing nonsensically as toddlers do, clapping his wet hands.

Happier times.

McGowan threw back half the drink. Immediately, he was glad she'd insisted. The liquor loosened his tightly wound nerves if only slightly.

He turned around reluctantly and walked around the big desk, set his glass down on the cluttered table, and sat back down in the chair. He looked at Renee slouched in the chair on the other side of the table.

A shrewd smile tugged at her lips, but there was a hard ferocity in her eyes. The old man had eyes like that. His hadn't been gray, but they, too, could change as quickly as the Rocky Mountain weather.

She blinked those hard, uncompromising eyes once,

slowly, and said, "He's dead, isn't he?"

A cold stone dropped in McGowan's belly. He kept his gaze on hers. He drew a breath, licked his upper lip, feeling the prickling of his mustache against his tongue. He frowned curiously. "How…?"

"Why else would you nearly kill your horse? To get back from town before anyone else had opportunity to tell me." Almost casually, her hand shaking only a little, she lifted the glass to her lips and took a deep drink of the bourbon. She lowered the glass to her right thigh, and that cold smile curled one half of her upper lip, which trembled a little, briefly. "You needed to be the one…"

"I did, boss. I needed to be the one."

She sucked a sharp breath, lifted her chin, and hardened her voice. "Who murdered my son, Garth?"

Again, he frowned. "How did you…?"

"Know he was murdered? It's in your eyes." Again, she sipped her drink but kept her eyes on his. Her hand shook a little more this time. That was her only display of emotion.

It chilled him.

"You're afraid, Garth. You were afraid to tell me. If had been an accident, there wouldn't be that fear in your cowardly eyes."

"Please, boss…"

"Who, Garth?"

64

He took a quick sip of his own drink, but it did nothing to steady his nerves this time. "Look, boss...he robbed the bank. Him and two others, those two jaspers he's been runnin' with..."

"The bank." It wasn't a question. She was saying it aloud to absorb the information, lifting her chin still farther, tilting her head back, her eyes showing a cold shrewdness and a grave understanding.

"He was shot in the bank?"

"No, he was shot out on the trail. A couple days ago."

"By who?"

"Some bounty hunter."

"*Who?*"

McGowan studied her, the fear growing in him, pooling in his belly like hot water. This was where he'd known the conversation was going, and he'd also known he needed to send it off on a different track. This was dangerous territory they were getting into now. This was powder-keg territory. This was the territory where everything he and the old man had worked so hard for died.

And the kid wasn't worth it.

"Does it matter, boss? They killed two posse members—Bill Ryder and Jem Clifton."

"Useless scoundrels, both. My father fired Bill Ryder years ago for the way he looked at me!"

McGowan knew her well enough to know that she'd loved how Bill Ryder had looked at her. And she'd loved that her father had fired him for looking at her that way. "I know, but still…"

"Did Weldon kill them?"

McGowan scowled and shrugged, a desperation rising in him. "They don't know who killed them. The posse didn't see who fired. The robbers fired from bushwhack. Apparently, the bounty hunter had no choice but to shoot Weldon. It was self-defense."

"Weldon wasn't good with a gun. You know that. In fact, he was frightened of guns!"

"Well, I know, but…" Well, he did not know, but he was too cowardly to tell her that he'd heard the kid had gotten right handy with a rifle over the past couple of years. Even handy with a hogleg, which he'd worn tied down on his leg though never around his mother.

"He robbed a bank. *Her* bank! And for *that*, they killed my *son*?" She leaned forward, pressing her open hand against her freckled cleavage. "I want to know who killed him. His name, Garth!"

"Henry's his name. Yakima Henry. Half-breed Injun." McGowan threw back the rest of his drink then rose and headed back to the liquor cabinet to refreshen his glass.

He desperately didn't want to tell her the rest, but he had no choice. She'd find out sooner or later, and she'd hold his not telling her against him. She'd know what he feared in her, what he feared she'd do. And that in and of itself might make her do it.

When he'd poured more whiskey into his glass, he carried the decanter back over to her. Without looking at him, but staring wordlessly at the coffee table, she held her empty glass out over the chair arm, and he refilled it.

"Yakima Henry," she said very quietly, staring down at the coffee table. "Half-breed bounty hunter…" She looked up at McGowan again, and the coldness in those gray eyes froze the marrow in his bones.

He set his replenished glass and the decanter on the coffee table then sagged back down in the chair. Leaning forward, resting his elbows on his knees, he cleared his throat. "Look, boss…there's something more."

She'd returned her gaze to the coffee table but now she shifted her eyes to him, again wrinkling the skin above the bridge of her nose.

"Now, you have to understand, Renee—she didn't know who robbed her bank. Weldon an' the other two—they were all wearing masks. You know—flour sacks with the eyes and mouths cut out?" He raised his left index finger to his face as though to illustrate then felt foolish for doing so. It only betrayed his nervousness.

"Continue," she ordered.

"Ah, hell, boss." He reached for his glass, sipped,

then set it back on the coffee table. Thunder rumbled in the distance. He thought it fitting that a storm would roll in about now, the weather outside matching the weather inside.

Right fitting.

He lowered his head and ran is hands through his close-cropped hair, digging his fingers into his scalp as though to try to release the pressure building inside him. "She put out a reward."

"She did what?"

He smoothed his hair back down with both hands and looked up at her. "She put out a reward on the robbers. But only because she didn't know—"

Renee shook her head, narrowed her eyes. "She placed a bounty on my son's *head*?"

"Like I said..."

"Yes, I know what you said. Why are you making excuses for her, Garth?"

"Why...*what?* I'm not..."

"Are you in love with her?"

McGowan's lower jaw dropped in shock. "Of course not!"

"How could you not be? Every man in the county's in love with her!"

He would have said that every man in the county was in love with both of them, but that wouldn't have helped anything. It would have only muddied the waters. He had to settle her down, not argue with her.

He slid forward, shoved the coffee table out of his way, and dropped to his knees before her. Again, thunder rumbled, a deep booming sound. Closer this time.

McGowan placed his hands on her thighs, not knowing and not caring that it might get him a hard slap across the face. You never knew with her. She could make love to you one minute and threaten to fire you the next minute for leaving manure on the porch steps.

He dug his fingers into her thighs, feeling the rigidness in her otherwise supple body, and let his desperate gaze bore into hers. "Renee, you've lost your son. I know how you feel. I know how you felt about Weldon. But he robbed the bank...ambushed a posse...and now he's dead. It's nobody's fault. It's not *her* fault. Hell, it's not even the bounty hunter's fault. He was just..."

"...doing his job," Renee finished for him. "He was only collecting the bounty she'd placed on my son's head. And him a half-breed, no less!"

"She didn't know it was Weldon," he said, hearing the fear in his voice and feeling ashamed for his weakness, knowing she heard it there, as well, and would use it against him.

That's how Renee was. She probed her men for weakness and then used it against them...to get them to do her bidding.

She stared back at him, her eyes as hard as two gray stones.

But then suddenly her lips quivered. And then suddenly tears dribbled from her eyes and down her cheeks, and she was quietly sobbing, sitting there in the chair, shaking and sobbing.

Unexpectedly, this sudden display of grief touched him. He felt his heart swell for her.

What the hell did that mean?

He hadn't fallen in love with her, had he?

If he had, that would be the end of him.

He started to pull his hands up off her thighs but she reached for them quickly, placing them back down on her legs, pressing them down against her, her hands on his. She sobbed and ground his hands against her thighs.

Her head was down, her eyes closed, and she was crying, and he was marveling at her display of emotion. He'd just realized that though he'd worked at the Bear Track for twenty years, he'd never seen her cry.

Not even one time. Not even after Daniel had died.

"Oh, Garth!" She closed her hands around his, squeezing, and looked at him through the veil of her tears. "Take me upstairs. Please, Garth. Take me upstairs!"

"Oh...well...all right...all right..."

The order had hit him like a fist, but as she slid forward

in the chair, he took her into his arms, his right arm cradling her head, his left arm hooked under her knees. He rose with a grunt, holding her against his chest.

"Please, Garth!" she cried. "Upstairs!"

"All right, boss...all right, boss...."

He carried her out of the room and upstairs to the room in which she'd shot her husband.

***

It was like making love to a killer wildcat in a violent thunderstorm.

He'd never known such pain...such pleasure.

She clawed and bit him by turns and then she threw her head back and wailed until the windows rang in their frames.

It went on like that for hours, outside storming, inside storming. He made love to her and then he held her as she wailed and screamed, convulsing in his arms, her bereavement nudging her up close to the chasm of insanity. A few times he thought she went over the edge.

Then they made love again, sometimes gently, sometimes violently, and that seemed to pull her back out of the chasm and settle her down for a time.

Then back to the grief...the rage. Thunder drummed and lightning flashed in the windows...

Finally, she slept, their bodies curled together.

Carefully, he extricated himself from her desperate embrace, relieved he didn't wake her. Long scratches marked his arms and shoulders, and he could feel the burn of her fingernails all across his back. Some were bleeding. He found a towel, wiped the blood away, tossed the towel in a corner.

The thunder and lightning had moved on, but a light rain continued to pelt the windows. A soothing sound after the previous storms—the one outside, the one inside.

Quietly, he dressed then carried his boots downstairs.

In the foyer, he stepped into his boots then walked out onto the porch.

He wasn't sleepy. His nerves were too jangled, and a heavy darkness had settled over him, around him. He sat in a wicker chair and sat staring out into the rainy darkness. The pines dripped quietly, a peaceful, pleasant sound.

He'd sat there for maybe fifteen minutes when the doorlatch clicked and the big front door groaned open. He turned to see her step out onto the porch. She'd wrapped a blanket around herself. He could see through an opening in the blanket a long stretch of bare, freckled leg. Even in the darkness, her hair was a fireball about her head and creamy shoulders.

"Garth?" she said quietly as she walked toward him.

"Yes, boss?"

She sat down on his lap, squirmed against him. He could hear her breathing, feel the beating of her heart through her back. She rubbed her nose up taut against his neck then sat very still, her cheek resting against his shoulder.

"You'll kill him, won't you?" she asked.

McGowan drew a deep breath, pressed his hands down against her thighs, over the blanket.

"Anything for you, boss," he heard himself say. He hadn't known he'd say it, but of course he would.

What else could he do—him being who he was, her being who she was?

She lifted her head suddenly and looked into his eyes. "Not her." She shook her head. "Just him. Yakima Henry," she said, annunciating each word carefully, darkly.

She rested her cheek against his shoulder again. "She killed my husband. Now she's killed my son. I'm going to take care of her myself." Quietly, she added a few seconds later, "Kill the half-breed, Garth."

73

Chapter 7

Yakima found a quiet watering hole in which to enjoy a late supper of chili and beer while waiting out the storm that had rolled in just after dark. When the storm had rolled out, he tramped through the muddy streets, heading for the livery barn in which he'd housed Wolf after the Sarge had had the three dead bank robbers, including the kid, hauled off to an undertaking parlor.

Since he was short on cash and still needed trail supplies, he'd arranged with the livery barn's manager, a stout oldster named Flynn, to sleep in the barn with his horse. Now as he approached the barn's man door to the left of the two double stock doors, a soft female voice said, "Hello, Yakima."

He stopped dead in his tracks, his right hand automatically going to the horn grips of his holstered .44. He turned to see Pearl O'Malley step out from behind the barn's front left corner, the flickering orange light from an oil pot burning out front of a nearby hurdy gurdy house delineating her slender female figure in wool shirt and denim trousers, straight flaxen hair tumbling down from her bullet-crowned cream hat.

In the male garb she filled out so nicely, he'd be damned if she didn't remind him of a fetching young lady he'd known in Apache Springs awhile back.

"Jesus, Pearl," Yakima said. "You're gonna get yourself shot skulkin' up on a fella like that!"

"I wasn't *skulkin'* up on you," she said, crossing her arms under her breasts and leaning up against the barn's front wall near the corner. "I was waiting for you."

"It's late. You should be in bed."

"So should you."

"Yeah, well, I was. Then I got hungry…thirsty." The truth was, the dead kid had haunted him, kept him from falling asleep. Not just the kid but the whole dirty business of who he was, not to mention the danger Yakima had put Beatriz Salazar in when he'd killed the kid despite the fact that she herself had placed the bounty on his head.

Yakima reached for the handle of the door before him. "Good night, Pe—"

"How are you, Yakima?"

He stopped with his hand on the door handle and turned to the pretty girl, frowning with annoyance. "What?"

She pushed off the barn and strode slowly toward him, her arms still crossed beneath her breasts, pushing them up enticingly. "How are you?"

"I'm fine."

Pearl stopped before him, uncrossed her arms and placed her right hand on his left forearm, probing the corded muscles with her fingers. She gazed up at him, concern in her eyes that reflected the wavering red light from the oil pot. "Are you? You were led into a whipsaw. It's not fair. You're having to leave so soon, too. It's not fair. We could get to know each other."

Yakima gave a caustic laugh. "I think your pa would have something to say about that, young lady. Now if you'll forgive…"

He pulled the man door open. She tightened her grip on his arm and said, "Pa's asleep. Went to bed with a bottle. What he doesn't know won't hurt him. You shouldn't be alone tonight. Me, neither. Pa's stranglehold on me makes it kind of lonely, if you know what I'm sayin'."

Yakima turned to her again, offered a gentle smile of understanding. "You'll meet the right guy soon, Pearl. Someone your pa approves of. That fella isn't me. You go on home, now, hear?"

She released his arm, gazed up at him as she pulled her mouth corners down. "You're no fun at all!"

Yakima chuckled then stepped through the man door

and drew it closed behind him. He stood at the door, lowering his head and pricking his ears. When Pearl's retreating footsteps had dwindled to silence, he sighed in relief though the damage had been done. He felt the old male pull down deep in his belly, the constriction of desire in his throat.

He hadn't had a woman for a long time. He'd been on the trail alone a long time, and a man had desires.

Cursing, he turned up the wick on a lamp hanging from a ceiling support post, walked to the barn's front corner, peeled back half of the hinged wooden lid over the water barrel, and dunked his head in the brackish water, opening his mouth and drawing like a horse. Shaking the water from his hair, he tramped down the alley to the stable in which Flynn had housed Wolf.

Yakima opened the stable door and had to push the heavy beast to one side, grunting with the effort, to make room for himself. Wolf nosed him, whickering. Yakima cradled the sleek snout in one arm and rubbed his nose against the horse's with deep affection. He loved the horse, and the horse loved him.

"Did you miss me, you old broomtail?"

The horse whickered again, fluttered his lips and twitched his ears.

Yakima kicked up some straw in a corner of the stall, doffed his hat, removed his gun and cartridge belt, coiled the belt around the gun, and dropped the rig into the mounded straw. He kicked out of his boots and fell into the hay, yawning and saying, "Don't stomp on me when you're dreamin' about the fillies, now, dammit!"

He chuckled again, fell back into the straw and, after the food and the beer, was almost instantly out.

Instantly out and dreaming.

In the dream, the stable door opened, and Yakima looked up to see his beloved Faith enter the stall, her blond hair limned by the light of a late-rising moon angling through a near window.

"Faith," he said, that constriction tightening his throat once more.

Wolf whickered a heartfelt greeting of his own. Wolf had missed her, too.

She smiled one of her trademark beguiling smiles and moved toward him. She was barefoot, he saw in the moonlight, and was wrapped in a striped trade blanket. When she dropped the blanket, she stood before him— cream-skinned, high-busted, and not wearing a stitch.

He couldn't get out of his own clothes fast enough. She helped him, laughing, and then she shoved him back in the hay and straddled him.

Her dangling silky hair tickled his broad chest and his shoulders as she toiled above him, her breasts in his hands.

After they'd shuddered together in their final throes, she lay sweating and panting against him, nuzzling his neck. Suddenly, she lifted her head and swept her flaxen hair back from her face with her arm and gazed down at him. It was then that he realized he hadn't been dreaming.

It wasn't Faith he'd made love to. Who'd made love to him, rather.

It was Pearl.

"I'd best get back home, darling," Pearl said with a sly smile, her eyes glittering in the moonlight. She rubbed her nose against his, kissed his lips. "Thank you for that, big man. I had a feelin' you'd change your mind." She frowned. "By the way, who's Faith?"

Gazing up at her, stunned but somehow still aroused by the fiery, lovely, young she-cat, her pale, pink-tipped breasts heaving in front of his face, he cleared the frog from his throat and tried to speak but couldn't find the words to convey his surprise as well as his disenchantment at not finding Faith here with him, but this off-limits young woman.

Still, he had to admit, he'd had fun...

And there was no way this had been her first time. No, despite her father's restrictions, Pearl O'Malley had been well tutored in the ways of love.

"Never mind," Yakima said.

"Silly man. You're still half asleep, aren't you?" Pearl

giggled as she raked his lips playfully with her index finger, kissed him again, climbed to her feet, and wrapped the blanket around her forbidden body after giving him one more good look at it.

She cradled Wolf's snout in her arm, kissed it, and turned to Yakima once more. "Be careful on the trail, Yakima. She'll send killers for you. You can bet the seed bull on that."

She raked her bare toes down his chest to his lower belly, smiled, blew him a parting kiss, and left.

***

An hour later, at dawn, Yakima swabbed egg yolk and bacon grease from his plate in the Hi-Lo Café with a last remaining scrap of his baking powder biscuit and stuffed the biscuit into his mouth.

As he did, he spied movement out the window on his left. He turned to see Beatriz Salazar pull a smart-looking, canopied, leather-seated carriage up to the boardwalk fronting the restaurant. As the woman reined in the handsome Morgan in the traces, she glanced across her right shoulder, and her brown-eyed gaze locked with Yakima's.

She turned her head back forward, set the wagon brake, and climbed down out of the carriage. She was dressed in a black satin gown with a black satin waistcoat and a white silk blouse with a ruffled front. She wore a round, black felt hat adorned with a black feather rising from its black silk band. As she walked around behind the chaise, Yakima followed her with his curious gaze. His gaze left the woman to find the pine coffin riding in the back of the carriage.

Staring at the unexpected wooden overcoat, Yakima heard himself mutter, "What in God's name...?"

When he heard the bell over the café's front door rattle, he turned his head to stare over his shoulder toward the front of the place. The female banker stepped into the café and immediately walked toward him. There were only a few other people in the café, as it was still early, but every head turned toward her and followed her every step, mouths moving as the onlookers muttered their incredulity.

Of course, by now the nature of their association—the pretty bank president and the lowly half-breed—had been spread far and wide. Miss Salazar had a black reticule dangling from her left wrist, and she carried a brown leather valise in her right hand, tucked against her side.

"Mister Henry," she greeted him coolly, stopping at his table, "may I sit down? I'd like a word."

Yakima slid his empty plate away and drew his coffee cup, which the place's lone waitress had just refilled, toward him. "Have it your way," he said, kicking out the chair on the opposite side of the table. "I don't see how as we have much to discuss, though. Besides, not a safe place to be."

"Where isn't?"

"Anywhere near me."

She drew her mouth corners down then sat in the chair Yakima had kicked out. As she set the valise and the reticule on the table then slid her chair forward, she said, "You are no less safe in my company than I am in yours."

"Tricky situation for both of us, I reckon." Yakima canted his head toward the chaise parked out the window on his left. "Can I ask you just where in hell you're taking that? I assume the kid's body is in that wooden overcoat out there."

"It is," she said, then waved off the waitress who'd approached the table, very tentatively, to take her order. "I'm taking him home to his mother."

"You sure that's wise?"

She arched her brown brows in surprise. Her dark-brown hair hung in rich, recently brushed waves down her shoulders, glinting in the light of a near lantern. There were a few strands of gray in it, but they gave it a depth, a richness, as did the very fine age lines around her mouth and eyes. Her hair, mostly chocolate brown, contrasted nicely with the deep black of her waistcoat and skirt.

"Oh," she said. "You must have heard the story..."

"A bird told me."

"O'Malley," she said. "That old drunk never was one to keep his mouth shut."

"Sounds to me like he's done pretty well by you and your old friend, Renee. Don't blame Sarge. We're old friends, and I practically had to pry it out of him. I thought I deserved to know the, um, *complexity* of the situation, since it sounds like I've made one very formidable enemy in Renee Stratton. It's always nice to know how motivated the person is who's out to put a bullet in you. Sounds like I'll be looking over my shoulder for a while."

"Don't try to make me pity you, Mister Henry. I have a feeling you're rather accustomed to looking over your shoulder. Am I right?"

Yakima just stared back at her. She was right. Time to stow the self-righteous indignation.

She shook her head quickly. "I didn't come to talk about Renee." She unzipped the valise, withdrew a letter-sized manilla envelope, and slid it across the table toward Yakima. "This is the cash I owe you. I want you to take it."

"Don't want it."

"You earned it," she said, a flush of anger rising in her olive cheeks.

"It's blood money."

She laughed without mirth. "All bounty money is

blood money!"

Yakima extended a finger at the envelope. "That seems a little bloodier, somehow. Killing a kid for a woman who, it turns out, is a blood enemy of the kid's mother for fairly understandable reasons."

"How dare you judge me!" she said, not bothering to keep her voice down and thus attracting more stares. "You're a *bounty hunter*. Besides, earlier this morning, when I went over to fetch Weldon's body from the undertaker's, I saw young Miss O'Malley leave the livery barn dressed in nothing more than a blanket. She looked rather flushed, I might add. Don't tell me you weren't her reason for visiting the livery barn. Her reason for looking flushed."

"How'd you know I holed up in the livery barn?"

"Because I saw Pearl leaving it, and I saw the way she looked at you yesterday on the street. Don't tell me she was there to visit Mister Flynn."

Yakima averted his gaze and felt his ears warm with chagrin. *Boy*, he told himself. *I really need to pull my picket pin!*

When he looked up again, he saw her regarding him with a very faint smile in her eyes. He frowned, curious.

"A bounty hunter who blushes," she observed.

"One with a heart and one who blushes," Yakima said. "Now you've seen it all."

Miss Salazar reached across the table to nudge the envelope closer to him. "Take it."

"On one condition."

She arched a brow over a wide, brown eye.

"You let me ride out to the Bear Track with you this morning."

She jerked her head back in surprise. "Oh, no. That's out of the question!"

"The way I hear it, your riding out there with that kid's body is likely suicide."

Miss Salazar shook her head. "Renee won't kill me. That would be too easy. Besides, she lives to hate me. Now, you, on the other hand, she will likely kill. She has men who can do it. Every man she hires knows how to handle a gun. She learned that hiring practice from her father."

Yakima slid the envelope toward her.

She watched his hand. She drew a deep breath then lifted her eyes to his.

"All right," she said, sliding the envelope back across the table again. "At least you'll have money to pay for your own funeral."

Chapter 8

"Why are you doing this?"

It was the first time Beatriz Salazar had spoken after she and Yakima had left town nearly an hour ago, riding southwest through the rolling foothills of the Sawatch Mountains toward the Bear Track Ranch. Beatriz drove the carriage with a light hand on the reins while Yakima sat to her right. The golden morning sunshine glistened in her hair, the breeze jostling it and the feather in her hat.

Yakima shrugged a shoulder. "I killed him. Why shouldn't I do it? Explain what happened, why I had to kill him. He left me no choice."

"It won't make a difference."

"Maybe not, but I don't believe in running from my troubles. Or having a woman riding out to settle up for me."

She laughed derisively. "This woman wasn't riding out to settle up for you. I was riding out to settle up for me. At least, to deliver his body and get the confrontation that I know is coming over with."

"Well, whatever in hell I'm doing…or you're doing…I couldn't just ride away and leave you holding the bag, so to speak."

"A bounty hunter with a heart, who blushes, and who has a sense of honor."

He turned to see her looking at him again, that vaguely admiring light in her lovely eyes. "I wish you'd quit callin' me a bounty hunter. I'm not one. Leastways, not usually. I just needed some fast money to fund the winter in Old Mexico, and I figured going after those bank robbers would be a good way to make some. Little did I know…" he added with a fateful sigh.

"Yes, little did you know you would get mixed up in a bitter feud between two headstrong women."

"Touche."

Yakima glanced at her. "Were you fond of the kid?"

Beatriz shook her head. "When he was younger… and sweeter."

"The way you looked at him yesterday…"

She turned those soft, brown eyes to him. "It wasn't Weldon I was thinking of." She turned her head forward and changed the subject quickly. "If you're not usually a bounty hunter, what are you usually, Mister Henry?"

"I don't like the sound of Mister Henry, either. Why

don't you call me Yakima?"

"For now, it's Mister Henry," she said firmly, with a slow, resolute blink of her eyes.

"Have it your way." Yakima drew a deep breath, chuckling. "What am I usually? Good question. Usually, I drift from here to there. I work for a time—odd jobs, mostly, some ranch work, I've been a town lawman—and then I drift again."

She favored him with a forlorn look. "Must be a lonely life. No woman? No family?"

"No woman. Not anymore."

"What happened?"

Yakima turned to her, crooked an ironic smile. "Long story." He turned his head back forward to gaze out over the Morgan's twitching ears, last night's dream touching him again with that old, aching sadness.

"I see."

"What about you? No man?"

"No man," she said with a sigh.

"Never?"

"Never."

He glanced at her again. "How come?"

She glanced back at him with her own ironic smile. "Long story."

Yakima smiled his understanding.

He looked around at the low, rolling hills carpeted in

brome and wheat grass and peppered with cedars and pinion pines. "How much farther?"

"A mile or so. The headquarters is just beyond those trees up there."

Yakima gazed ahead along the trail which cut through an evergreen forest shaped like an arrowhead and angling down from the side of a tabletop mesa ahead and to his right. He spied movement in the corner of his left eye and turned to see the hind end of a horse and the vest-clad back of a rider just then drop down the far side of a low, tawny bench, quickly disappearing from view.

"I think we're being watched," he told Beatriz.

"Bet on it."

Yakima glanced at her.

"You can also bet that she knows we're coming by now."

"Eyes everywhere, eh?"

"On Bear Track, yes. She has eyes everywhere. By now, too, she's likely heard the news."

Yakima nodded slowly.

"If she hadn't gotten word we're coming, we likely would have met up with her along the trail by now. She would have been heading to town to pick Weldon up herself, with several gun-handy men in tow." Beatriz glanced at Yakima. "But now that she has received word from one of her riders, she will sit tight and let us come to her. She knows I know she knows, and she is enjoying that aspect of it, at least."

Yakima gave her a dubious look. Strange relationship, these two women.

Again, she glanced at Yakima. "Let me do the talking. I know how to handle Renee."

Yakima kept his eyes forward as he shook his head slowly, obstinately. "You speak for yourself. I'll speak for myself."

She arched her brow again and smiled. "A prideful man, as well."

"Yeah, well, aside from my horse, it's about all I have." As they entered the sun-dappled shade of the forest, the aromatic fragrance of pine touching Yakima's nostrils, he turned to her again. "I know it's none of my business, but..."

He let the sentence dwindle on his tongue when she turned to him, her eyes suddenly sharp with remonstration. "I know what you're going to ask me—why did I sleep with him—and you're right. It's none of your business."

"Sorry."

"Don't be. Everyone wonders. To be honest, I wonder myself."

He turned to see her gazing pensively into the forest on the right side of the trail.

As they started to leave the woods and head back into the blazing sunshine, three riders appeared sitting their horses in the trail maybe fifty yards ahead, facing Yakima and the woman.

"Whoa," she said, drawing lightly back on the Morgan's reins, stopping the horse.

The three riders gazed stonily toward her and Yakima—three hard-faced men in range gear including vests and chaps. All three had two pistols holstered on their hips or thighs.

The middle rider blinked slowly then said, "Come on," to the two others, and reined his horse around. The other two turned their own mounts, and all three men put their horses into trots, heading up trail.

Yakima and Beatriz shared a darkly conferring look then Beatriz shook the reins over the Morgan's back. "Gidup, there, boy."

As they followed the riders around a bend in the trail that wound around the belly of a steep, low ridge rising on his left, Yakima glanced down at the carriage floor, where he'd stowed his Yellowboy repeater in its saddle sheath.

He doubted it would do him much good. Beatriz had told him that Renee Stratton had a good twenty men on her payroll, all of them gun handy. But he would have felt naked coming without it. He'd have been stupid coming without it, too. Now, he had the rifle, his .44, his Arkansas toothpick, and his words.

Certainly, even a woman who sounded as uncompromising as Renee Stratton would listen to reason. Certainly, she'd realize after she'd heard his story that he'd had no choice but to shoot her son. After all, the kid had tried to bushwhack him from outside the cave. It had been three against one.

It had not been a personal thing. He'd simply been returning the kid's own fire.

If she did not listen to reason and it came to shooting, at least he was armed. He'd likely die, but he'd diminish Miss Stratton's payroll by a goodly number. Besides, he'd lived long enough.

Long enough without Faith.

He wasn't suicidal, and he did not want to die. But death held no fear for him.

He glanced at Beatriz who turned toward him and gave him a dark little half-smile, as though she'd been reading his mind.

And then they followed the three riders through the open gate and under the portal with the Bear Track brand burned into it and into the impressive yard of the Bear Track headquarters. A big log lodge sat off to the right, shaded by several tall pines. The bunkhouse, barn, stable, corrals, and blacksmith shop formed a slow, broad curve to the left of the house, a good sixty or seventy yards of hard-packed, hay- and straw-strewn yard away.

Those buildings were also shaded by pines.

To Yakima's left now as she halted the carriage, in a large corral connected to another corral by a narrow chute, five or six cowboys were branding what appeared to Yakima's eyes as yearling calves. Probably mavericks from last year recently rounded up. The calves were grouped in a corner of the corral, bawling. A fire burned, heating the branding iron, which was just now pressed to the behind of another hogtied calf, which kicked up a great screaming fuss.

The smell of scorched hide touched Yakima's nostrils.

The cowboys holding the calf down released the rope, and the calf went running and bawling through a chute into the far corral, where the already branded other calves milled, singing dirges to their scorched rear ends.

Yakima turned to where a good dozen or so other men stood gathered in a loose group in front of the L-shaped bunkhouse ahead and on his left. They stood silently staring at Yakima and the woman beside him.

Yakima looked at the three riders who'd stopped their horses just ahead of him. The oldest one, who appeared their leader, hipped around in his saddle to look at Yakima. He gave a hard, openly jeering smile as he canted his head toward the lodge. Yakima shuttled his gaze that way and saw a woman with flame-red hair and a tall, mustached gent in a high-crowned tan

Stetson standing atop the porch, gazing over the porch rail toward Yakima and Beatriz.

The woman wore a dark-blue shawl about her shoulders. Her long, thick, curly red hair blew in the breeze, flashing like copper in the sunlight.

Yakima glanced at Beatriz. She stared gravely back at Renee Stratton.

Beatriz flicked the reins, and the Morgan continued to the lodge and stopped near one of the two wrought-iron hitch racks standing to either side of the porch's broad, halved-log front steps.

Renee Stratton, a small but lush-bodied woman with pale, freckled skin, continued to stare down at Beatriz through her astonishingly expressive and direct gray eyes. She was every bit as beautiful in her own Irish way as was Beatriz in her Spanish fashion. Each woman could have set the standard for beauty in their respective races and ages. Also, their eyes were large and bold. Except, unlike those of Beatriz, Renee's were hard as cast-iron, and cold.

At the same time, both women gave the impression of great emotion raging inside the hearts of the owners of those eyes. Quietly raging emotion but raging emotion just the same.

Staring up at the unmoving couple on the porch, Beatriz raised her voice to say, "Renee, may I step down?"

Renee and the man just stood staring over the porch rail at them.

Yakima heard slow footsteps behind him. He turned to see men walking toward the lodge. It appeared that the three men who'd ridden in ahead of him and Beatriz and all of the men who'd been milling in front of the bunkhouse were heading toward the lodge. The only ones who were not were the five cowboys working with the calves.

A little snake of uneasiness writhed in Yakima's belly.

Beatriz turned toward the men moving toward the carriage and the lodge. Fear shone in her eyes. She turned her head back to the lodge and said, louder, "Renee, let me step down. I want to come up there and talk to you. I am sorry Weldon is dead, but..."

She stopped and turned back to the men approaching the carriage, fifteen feet away now and closing, obvious looks of menace glinting in their eyes, all of which were fastened on Yakima.

Beatriz whipped her head back toward the redhead staring stonily down at her through those odd gray eyes that had glints of tan in them. "Renee! Call them off!"

When the nearest man was ten feet away from the carriage, appearing to make a bee-line for Yakima, Yakima reached under the seat for his sheathed Winchester. He ripped it out of its sheath and gained his feet, cocking it and swinging it around toward the crowd of savage-eyed men closing on him.

"I have nine rounds in this long gun, Mrs. Stratton!" he said, keeping his eyes on the crowd of men that had suddenly stopped walking but continued staring at him with dark menace. "I know you have more men than that, but I've got a bullet for nine men!" He glanced up at the redhead now staring down at him. "We come in peace. Now hear us out!"

Silence.

Then, as Yakima heard footsteps coming up behind him as he faced the Bear Track men gathered now at the rear of the carriage, Beatriz cried, "*Yakima!*"

He tried to swing around but he made it only halfway before a broad loop dropped over his head and shoulders and drew instantly taut, pinning his arms and rifle against his sides, causing his index finger to squeeze back on the trigger.

The rifle thundered, making Yakima's ears ring.

He heard a windy rustle, and then another broad loop dropped around him, drawing taut, putting even more pressure on his arms. Just as he turned his head to see the two men who'd somehow snuck up around him grinning and holding coiled riatas, keeping up the tension in the rope extending between them and Yakima. All at once, they jerked back suddenly.

Yakima was pulled off his feet and over the front wheel of the carriage to hit the ground on his head and shoulders.

Stars burst behind his eyes.

"What the order, boss?" one of Yakima's two attackers yelled up at the porch.

"*Brand him!*" the redhead screamed at the tops of her lungs.

Chapter 9

The redhead's shrill scream echoed inside of Yakima's head as he fought to remain conscious on the ground beside the carriage.

"*Brand him!*"

Cold terror was the only thing keeping him from passing out.

Beneath the ringing in his ears that had kicked up when he'd met the ground so suddenly and violently, Yakima heard Beatriz scream, "Renee, stop this right now! We came here in peace to bring you Weldon's body and to explain what happened!"

"I know what happened," Renee returned. "You and your half-breed bounty hunter murdered my son!"

Her voice was growing louder. It was accompanied by slow foot thuds.

Groaning against the misery his tumble from the carriage had kicked up in his head, neck, and back, Yakima looked up to see the redhead moving down the porch steps beside the beefy, mustached man whom Yakima decided was her foreman and probably more. They were arm in arm, moving with a bizarre, intimate formality, their eyes cold, faces implacable.

Renee looked at the two men holding the ropes taut around Yakima then returned her lunatic gaze to her captive on the ground. "Didn't you hear me? Take him over to the fire and brand him!"

"You heard the boss, boys!" said the man descending the steps with her, giving a quick wave of his arm.

"You got it!" said one of the men holding the riatas taut around Yakima.

"No!" Beatriz had climbed down from the buggy and knelt over Yakima, gritting her teeth as she desperately tried to dig her hands under the ropes to free him.

"Grab her!" Renee shouted.

"I got her, boss!" Then a man was crouched over Yakima, grabbing Beatriz and pulling her up and away from him.

Beatriz screamed as she struggled against him, trying to kick him and to pry his thick arms clad in checked wool out from around her waist, her hair whipping around her head, obscuring her face.

Yakima struggled desperately against the ropes. The

notion of enduring the savagery of a branding had kicked up a wild fury mixed with terror inside him. As he fought against the ropes, he tried to slide his right hand to his gun, but the ropes were too tight. He couldn't move his hand more than an inch or two.

"Get that gun out of his holster!" yelled the man with Renee.

"I got it!"

By now, all of the Bear Track riders had closed around Yakima. One of them stepped forward, and Yakima felt the chilling lightening of his holster as his Colt was ripped out of it. That was followed by the *snicking* sound of his Arkansas toothpick being pulled out of the sheath on his other hip.

"Get up, you mangy half-breed dog!" ordered one of the two men holding the ropes taut around him. "Gonna take a little walk!"

"Go to hell!" Yakima said in a pinched voice quavering with fear and fury.

Keeping his rope taut, the man who'd spoken had moved up to within a few feet of where Yakima struggled on the ground by the carriage. Yakima grinned savagely as he rolled onto his left shoulder and hip and then swung both of his feet quickly in a scissoring motion from side to side. The man holding the rope near Yakima screamed as his own feet were cut out from beneath him.

He struck the ground on his back with a yelp, dropping the rope.

"Denford, you fool!" said the man holding the other rope, four feet to the right of where Denford now lay in a groaning heap.

With a new-found energy birthed by panic, Yakima shot up onto his knees and then to his feet. Hardening his jaws and gritting his teeth, he ran forward, taking two long, enraged strides, and bulled into the man holding the other rope, slamming his forehead against the rope holder's forehead. Yakima could feel the concussion of the powerful blow down deep in his neck and shoulders.

The man gave a clipped scream as he fell back, instantly rendered unconscious by the savage assault.

He struck the ground on his back, Yakima on top of him.

The other men shouted as they converged on Yakima.

Feeling the rope's slackness around his chest, Yakima quickly spread his arms. Rising to his knees, he flung both ropes over his head and then he ripped the ivory-gripped Colt from the holster of the man who lay unconscious on the ground before him. Just as he started to raise the hogleg, however, something hard and unforgiving slammed against the back of his head.

Rifle butt, no doubt.

His lights instantly dimming, Yakima dropped the

Colt and sagged forward, trying desperately to stay conscious and to keep from falling. The wild stallion of terror galloping inside of him knew what it would mean if he failed.

Branding...

He shook his head to clear the cobwebs. It didn't help much. He had just started to lift himself up off his knees when a man flung himself into him, slamming him back down on the ground and onto the man Yakima had head butted. Then another man was on top of him, lying across his legs, holding him down. And then there was a whole horde of men surrounding him, shouting, cursing, grunting, grabbing his arms...his legs...his hair...pinning him down.

"Get a horse over here!" Yakima recognized the voice of the man with the redhead—her foreman, her lover. "If he wants to make it so hard, we'll *drag* him over to the fire!"

Beneath the din of the shouting men around him, Yakima could hear the pleas and cries of Beatriz Salazar somewhere beyond the terrorizing Bear Track riders. When he was thrust onto his back while being pinned down by at least five sweaty, smelly Bear Track men, not having the strength enough to fight back after the clubbing, he looked up through the wash of men around him, the sea of range hats and wool shirts and neckerchiefs and gloved hands and chaps worn over denim. He locked gazes with the redhead, Renee Stratton.

She smiled down in grim satisfaction at him, her left arm hooked through the arm of the big, mustached man standing beside her.

If you brand me, I'll kill you, you bitch, Yakima tried to say but it was as though he were dreaming and trying to speak around a mouthful of rocks.

The redhead's eyes slid down Yakima's legs to his feet. Yakima followed her gaze and felt another pang of cold, wet terror as he watched a rope being wound and knotted tightly around his ankles. And then he was thrust onto his belly. His arms were hooked around behind his back. He felt the rough hemp of another rope being wrapped and knotted around his wrists.

"All right—let him go, boys!" one of the attackers shouted.

They all leaped away from Yakima as though from a calf that had just been branded. Yakima looked up now to see a cream horse and a rider maybe ten feet away from him. The horse was curveted away from him, its cream tail arched. A rope extended from Yakima's bound ankles to the horn of the cream's saddle.

The man on the horse was thick-set and red-mustached. He wore a brown work shirt, black vest, and high-crowned black hat. His pale blue eyes twinkled in delight as, hipped around in the saddle, the rope stretching across his bulging belly to the horn in front of him, he gazed back toward Yakima on the ground behind him.

The thick-set man ripped the Stetson from his head, swatted it against his horse's right hip, and howled. The horse lunged forward in a long, leaping lunge, giving a startled whinny.

Yakima gritted his teeth as the horse jerked him forward, lifting his legs, his butt and his back raking painfully across the ground. The ground quickly pulled his shirt out of his pants, ripping it open and pulling it up above him where it trailed along the ground, exposing his longhandle-clad back.

Yakima ground his teeth in fury, in agony, as the horse's galloping back hooves scissored in the air before him, to each side of his raised legs. He felt the longhandle top split between his shoulder blades, exposing his bare flesh to the ground raking him like a washboard.

The dragging seemed endless but probably only a minute had passed before the horse was brought to an abrupt halt and Yakima slid forward, propelled by his own momentum, and went rolling up beside the horse's left rear hoof, coming to rest on his belly, panting, groaning.

He lifted his head, grunting and spitting grit from his lips, turning his head to see the other hands running toward him, whooping and hollering like jackals on the blood scent. Behind them came Renee Stratton and the tall, mustached foreman, walking formally, arm in arm, eyes stony.

Behind them, Beatriz knelt on the ground by the buggy. She was alone now, just kneeling there in defeat, staring toward Yakima, sobbing into her hands. Her dress was torn, her hair disheveled.

"I'll get the iron!" One of the hands ran past Yakima and over to where the branding iron lay in the fire fifteen feet away.

Yakima could smell the lingering scent of scorched cowhide and hot iron. That and the prospect of having the end of that iron pressed to his flesh made his guts recoil like cold snakes.

In desperation he rolled onto his back, struggling to free himself.

No doing. The ropes were tied so tight that he could no longer feel his hands or his feet. There was no give in the hemp. They'd cut into his wrists; blood oozed from the cuts. Fighting the ropes only made them bleed more but he couldn't stop himself.

"Bastards," he grunted as the crowd of whooping and hollering hands gathered around him. "You damned lousy bastards. If you do this—"

"You'll do *what*?"

"*Ghaahhh!*" Yakima's breath exploded out of him as

PETER BRANDVOLD

a boot was driven into his belly. He drew his knees to his chest in agony, grimacing.

"You're nothin' but a lowdown dirty half-breed son of a bitch!" wailed the man who'd kicked him, bending over to glare down at him. He was tall and hatchet-faced, and he wore a dusty black Stetson with a crow feather protruding from the braided rawhide brand. "Dirty low-down, *murderin'* half-breed son of a bitch!"

"You tell him, Crow!" howled one of the other savage attackers and laughed.

As he tried to suck a breath back into his chest, Yakima stared up at the man called Crow, etching the man's sallow, narrow face into his brain for later.

If there was a later...

He turned his head to see the crowd of ranch hands part for Renee and her foreman. The pair walked toward Yakima, gazing at him almost blandly.

"Who wants the honors?" said the hand who'd snatched the branding iron from the fire.

He was short and wiry with shoulder-length sandy hair, a soot-smudge mustache, and dung-brown eyes. He was possibly the youngest of the lot. Young, yes. But he'd die, too.

"I believe I deserve that privilege," said Renee said, releasing the foreman's arm and walking over to where the grinning kid held the branding iron high above his head.

As Renee approached him, the kid lowered the iron, handed it to her, then politely stepped back, deferentially bowing his head.

Renee lowered the iron to her side and walked over to stand near Yakima. Glaring down at him, her gray-tawny eyes glowing like the stones embedded in some dark totem, she commanded shrilly, "Hold him down and *strip him*!"

Yakima convulsed with rage and terror, gritting his teeth, fighting the ropes but feeling only more oily blood well from his cut wrists.

One man shoved Yakima brusquely onto his back and then, laughing and grunting, he ripped Yakima's tattered shirt from his shoulders. He ripped the longhandle top down to Yakima's waist. Then he knelt with both knees on Yakima's chest, still laughing, holding his victim down. The man's weight felt enormous, like that of anvil, punching the air out of Yakima's lungs.

The crowd of men howled and yipped like mad coyotes as another man hastily unbuckled Yakima's cartridge belt, removed it, and tossed it away. Because of the big man kneeling on his chest, Yakima couldn't see the other man ripping off his denims and his short, summer-weight underwear.

He could only feel the man's quickly moving, gloved, defiling hands until Yakima lay naked on the ground, the crowd gathered around him suddenly going quiet so that Yakima could hear the piping of birds indifferent to this spectacle.

One man chuckled.

Another whistled.

Yakima looked up to see his redheaded tormentor, Renee Stratton, gazing down at his exposed flesh. She widened her eyes as though in appreciation at what she saw just south of his belly then slid her gaze to Yakima's face, crooking a leering half-smile.

"I see what she sees in you, big man," she said, glancing back toward Beatriz who was still kneeling and sobbing by the carriage. "I'm going to put this brand where every lover from now on is sure to notice it, so that whenever you make love, you'll be reminded of this day...you'll be reminded whose brand you wear—and *why*!"

"*Don't do it, lady!*" Yakima warned, writhing feebly against the two men holding him down and the ropes binding him. "*Don't you do it, lady!*"

He suddenly felt the urge to beg, but he wouldn't do it. He'd never been driven this low, made to feel so small... so afraid...so desperate.

Again, she smiled coldly. Her glowing eyes were the eyes of a deranged Celtic warrior queen.

Renee stepped forward.

Teeth gritted, lips stretched back, Yakima stared in dread at the glowing Bear Track brand at the end of the iron she held in her right, black-gloved hand. White smoke licked up from around the glowing umber brand shaped like a bear paw.

Yakima grunted desperately. His body convulsed with panic, the chords in his neck standing out like taut ropes...

Because of the man kneeling on top of him, Yakima did not see the brand pressed against his upper thigh, just below belt level. He wasn't sure he felt it at all until it had been pressed there for a second or two. At first, it was an oddly subtle sensation. Almost like the kiss of a tender lover.

But then, when he heard the sizzling sound and smelled the odor of his own burning flesh, he felt as though the brand had been thrust down deep into his loins, melting the very marrow in his bones.

The last thing he heard before unconsciousness mercifully claimed him was his own agonized wails.

Chapter 10

Beatriz was relieved when the screams died.

On her knees in defeat by the carriage, she had her head down. She'd been grinding her forehead into the hard-packed dirt of the ranch yard as though to drown with her own pain the screams of the man being treated so cruelly down near the fire.

Now she lifted her head slowly, opened her eyes, and stared across the yard at the crowd of Bear Track men now slowly dispersing, chuckling, laughing, and casting looks back over their shoulders in satisfaction at their handiwork.

Renee and her foreman, Garth McGowan, stood gazing down at the unconscious man, Yakima Henry. Renee still held the branding iron over the bare leg she'd just blazed with her brand.

She'd given him something to remember her by.

More satisfying than killing him, in Renee's eyes.

As she gazed down at the unconscious victim of her savage torture, Renee moved her lips, saying something that Beatriz couldn't hear from this distance and above the drumming of her heart in her ears. Four men who'd lingered around Yakima now walked over to him. Each grabbed a leg or an arm, lifted him brusquely up off the ground, and began carrying him toward where Beatriz knelt by the carriage.

They carried him like they'd carry some animal they'd killed—carelessly.

Beyond them, Renee tossed the branding iron into the fire. She and McGowan began walking toward the house, following the four men carrying Yakima.

Slowly, heavily, still trembling from the horror of what she'd witnessed, Renee gained her feet. She watched the four men toss Yakima into the back of the carriage, again like some dead game animal, then slide the coffin out of the carriage. Each man holding a corner on his shoulder, they carried the coffin around Renee, none of them looking at her, and over to the house and up the broad porch steps.

Beatriz heard a groan rise from the back of the carriage.

She walked over to the rear of the chaise, stared down at the big, naked, copper-skinned man squeezing his eyes closed and writhing in pain. His disheveled, sweat-damp hair to which dirt and straw clung was sprayed across his shoulders and concealed part of his face. She winced when she saw the charred brand that had been burned into his upper left thigh.

He held his hand over it, squeezing, gritting his teeth.

"Hold on," she said. "I'll get a blanket."

She walked up to the front of the carriage and reached under the seat for the blanket she kept folded there. She turned to carry the blanket back to the rear of the chaise but stopped when she saw Renee and the foreman slowly approaching.

McGowan carried a rifle in his right hand, a holstered revolver and cartridge belt in his left hand, the belt coiled around the holster.

"These are his," the foreman told Beatriz. "I've emptied the hogleg and the long gun, but he can have them back. I'm no thief."

"How thoughtful," Beatriz said with a flair of a nostril.

McGowan set the holstered revolver and the rifle in the carriage beside the groaning Yakima then turned back to Beatriz. "Tell him if he's ever seen around here again, he'll die hard. He probably won't see it like this, but he's been given a gift here today. He's alive. Just tell him to light a shuck out of this country fast. If he's ever seen around here again, he will be a dead man."

He pinched his hat brim to Beatriz then walked over

to stand beside Renee.

As she turned to Renee, anger once more flared inside Beatriz, making her shoulders tremble. "You've done some crazy, terrible things, Renee. But this..." She shook her head slowly, still in shock over what she'd bore witness to. "This was not only uncalled for, it was savage. It was inhuman."

Renee smiled that cold, vacant smile of hers. "You've been given a gift, too, Beatriz. If you'd come alone, it would have been you wearing that brand. Since you brought him, my son's killer, I spared you, who sicced him on my boy! Live with that, Beatriz. Enjoy your unmarred flesh. You cost him his!"

So that was her punishment, Beatriz thought. Subtle but effective. She'd been made to watch the torture of the man who, in Renee's eyes, she'd sent after Weldon. And whom Renee assumed was Beatriz's lover. Now Beatriz would have to live with the guilt of his punishment, knowing he'd been her sacrificial lamb, so to speak.

Subtle but effective.

No doubt there would be more punishment later. But for now, Renee was satisfied. The man who'd killed her son would wear her mark for the rest of his life and remember the horror he'd lived through. Now Renee could go on hating the woman she saw as her life's nemesis.

Hating Beatriz gave her life meaning, something to crawl out of bed for every morning.

Beatriz watched Renee and McGowan walk slowly, arm in arm, over to the house, mount the porch steps, and walk inside.

"It must be nice to have a single person to blame all of your misfortunes on," she said quietly to herself.

She continued to the back of the carriage and draped the blanket over Mr. Henry. He was already beading with a fever sweat and shivering. As she tucked the blanket around him, his eyelids fluttered so that she could see the green of his eyes fleetingly between the lids as they reflected the high-country sunlight.

He appeared half-conscious.

"Don't worry," she said, "I'll get you out of here now, Yakima."

She hurried around to the front of the carriage, climbed inside, and unwrapped the reins from around the brake handle. She released the brake, turned the Morgan away from the house and urged him into a trot across the yard and through the open gate and portal.

Again, she trembled, remembering the agonized screams.

***

"Maybe should have killed him," McGowan said as he and Renee stepped into the house and he'd closed the door behind them.

"No," Renee said, shaking her head quickly. "This is better. To have to live with my mark is better."

"I don't know," McGowan said, feeling a strange unease. "When you do something like that to a man—"

"He remembers you," she finished for him. She looked up at him, crooking a smile as cold as the winds of a mountain winter. "I want him to remember me until the day he dies."

Boots thudded and McGowan turned to see the four hands who'd carried Weldon's coffin into the house walk toward him and Renee down the long, shadowy hall—big, lumbering men, their boots kicking up a thunder on the varnished wooden floors.

"We set him in the parlor just like you wanted, boss," said the hand named Lomax, a tall, beefy man with a pink knife scar angling down his thick neck to disappear under his shirt. He paused near Renee and the foreman and doffed his hat, held it over his heart. "Sure are sorry about your loss, Mrs. Stratton. Weldon...he'll...he'll sure be missed!"

The other three men hastily removed their own hats and muttered their agreements.

Silently, McGowan chuckled. The hell you're sorry.

The only one who's gonna miss that devil is his mother, who for some reason was never able to see into the boy's cold, black heart. Even colder than Renee's own.

The four hands set their hats back on their heads, stepped around Renee and McGowan, and headed outside and back to their assigned chores.

Staring toward the parlor where her son's coffin lay, Renee placed her hand on McGowan's arm. "Pour me a drink, Garth," she said with some urgency.

"You got it, boss. Comin' right up."

He doffed his own hat, pegged it, then stepped into the kitchen and strode over to the cupboard where she, like her father had, kept a good supply of liquor, mostly bourbon.

"Pour yourself one!" she called from where she remained in the foyer.

"Don't mind if I do." He set out a second glass and lifted the glass stopper from the decanter. "Don't mind if I do..."

That unease, like a premonition of bad things to come, stayed with him. He wished he hadn't given the breed's guns back to him, but that wouldn't have made a difference. The man could get his hands on another pistol and rifle easy enough. Besides, the Colt and the Winchester had belonged to him, and McGowan was no thief. He'd seen returning the weapons as the honorable thing to do.

He might have helped punish the man, but he was, by God, honorable.

He took the drinks back into the foyer, but Renee was no longer there. She must have gone into the parlor.

Wincing, wishing he could somehow avoid being here to witness her grief, especially since he had to pretend to share it, he walked down the shadowy hall, the whiskey sloshing in the glasses. He passed the old man's study where he and the old man had enjoyed many long conversations usually late at night and with bourbon and stepped into the parlor.

He stopped in the doorway.

Lomax and the other men had set the coffin atop the piano in the parlor's rear right corner, to the right of the fieldstone hearth. An old Texas flag was draped over the piano—had been for as long as McGowan could remember—and the coffin sat on that. Renee had removed the coffin's lid and leaned it against the piano, to her right. Standing with her back to McGowan, she stood staring down into the box.

She stood there for a long time, staring, then slowly turned her head to gaze over her left shoulder at the big man in the doorway. "Flesh of my flesh," she said forlornly. Ladder rung lines etched themselves across her freckled forehead. "And now he's gone."

McGowan strode forward, crossing the room to her, and held out the glass in his right hand. "Here."

Looking up at him, she put a little steel in her voice

as she said, "She's taken everything from me now. She took Daniel...and now she's taken my son." She turned her head to gaze down into the box in which the kid lay waxy and blue in death, hands crossed on his chest, his sightless eyes open and staring at nothing.

She turned her head to McGowan again and said, "And, still, I let her live. Why is that?"

McGowan drew a deep breath. "I don't know, boss— you two go back. You were girls together."

"We were best friends until she betrayed me."

He extended the drink again. "Here. Make you feel better."

She took the glass, took a halting, tentative sip, frowning, deep in thought. "What is it between her and me... that I can't kill her like I'd kill anyone else who had done what she's done to me?"

McGowan sipped his own drink. "I can't imagine you killin' Beatriz."

"No." Renee shook her head, frowning, deeply troubled. "Why...?" She looked up at him again, the question still in her eyes, probing him for the answer she seemed to need so terribly.

"I don't know," he said, wishing he could give her the answer she wanted but was unable to. "She's a powerful woman. A banker. If you killed her..."

"You think I'm afraid of the *law*?" She smiled as though

at the preposterousness of the thought.

He did not say what was on his mind: *The old man isn't here to save your behind this time. Maybe that's why you haven't killed her.*

Still frowning, she shook her head. "No, that's not it. Something, though. There's something…"

Suddenly, she turned to McGowan again, another question in her eyes. "You don't think…you don't think *she'll* come after *me*, do you?"

Her rich lips spread a broad smile, as though the notion delighted her. She snorted a devious little laugh.

"Nah," McGowan said, taking another sip of his whiskey. "She wouldn't do that. That's not her way."

The breed, though. Maybe should've killed him.

"I'll give you some time alone," he said, nodding toward the coffin.

He took another sip of the whiskey then turned and strode to the door.

"Don't stray far, Garth," she called when he was walking down the hall. "I'm going to need you later!"

He winced, still feeling the burn of her claw marks on his back.

Chapter 11

A wolf sunk its teeth into Yakima's left thigh and shook him, growling and snarling, tearing the flesh.

He woke with a start, lifting his head up sharply from the pillow.

"It's all right!" said Beatriz Salazar. "You're all right. I was just freshening the poultice."

She sat in a chair before him. He was in a bed. The covers were pulled back to expose his midsection. He was naked. She held a hand over a thick bandage resting atop his left thigh. Her face was turned toward his, her large brown eyes reflecting the soft light of a near lamp.

She wore a light wrap over a low-cut cotton nightgown. Her dark-brown hair spilled down her right shoulder. The wrap was open, exposing the upper planes of her breasts.

Her breasts swelled and rose as she drew a breath. She looked down, following Yakima's gaze, then drew the wrap closed, a flush rising in her cheeks.

Yakima looked around. He was in a bedroom, a nice one with simple but stylish furniture including the four-poster bed he was in, a dresser, a chest of drawers, and an armoire. The walls were papered, and a cabinet clock ticked woodenly on the wall to the left of the half-open door behind Beatriz. The clock showed it was around ten-thirty. Since Beatriz was in her nightgown, he assumed it was ten-thirty at night. He couldn't see the room's two windows because heavy velvet drapes were drawn over them.

"Where am I?"

"My house at the edge of Lone Pine."

Yakima looked down at his exposed privates.

"Sorry," she said and drew the covers over his crotch. "I assure you, I was only—"

"What's that smell?"

"Licorice root, moss, a few other things."

"Stinks."

"The few other things include whiskey and horse urine. A concoction of my father—an old Salazar family recipe." She smiled.

Yakima looked down at the poultice. "Let me see."

She shook her head. "Not yet."

"Let me see." Yakima laid his hand over hers, pried up her hand and the bandage covering the stinky poultice, which looked like green mud and moss and spider webs, too. He stared down in horror at his upper left thigh—the charred, red flesh in the shape of a bear's paw oozing puss. It was roughly as large around as his hand.

"Good Christ!"

"I'm sorry."

"You didn't do it. She did."

He removed his hand from hers, and she closed the bandage and poultice over the burn again. She reached for a roll of gauze on a small table to his left. "It will heal. We just have to keep it clean, keep infection out."

"Your friend's off her nut."

"If you mean Renee is insane, yes." Beatriz was wrapping the gauze around his leg, working very slowly and gently. "I never before realized just how insane she was." She looked down as she wrapped the gauze several times around his leg before cutting it off the roll with a small scissors and knotting it over the poultice.

She set the gauze and the scissors on the table and looked at him. "I want you to know I feel terribly about this. Just awful."

"You warned me."

"Still..." Gazing sadly into his eyes, she slowly shook her head.

Yakima placed his hand on one of hers, gave her an

understanding smile, and gently squeezed her hand reassuringly.

"We'll get you healed. Get you out of here. It's not safe—"

Yakima frowned. "Out of here?"

"Yes, it's not safe. She has spies. They both do—her and Garth McGowan, her foreman. They'll know if you haven't left in a couple of days."

Yakima removed his hand from hers. "Lady, I'm not goin' anywhere."

It was her turn to frown with incredulity. "What do you mean? You've seen how she is. How powerful she is. How many men she has."

"I've seen. A good twenty."

Beatriz raised and hardened her voice. "Please... you're not thinking."

"I won't run from her. Maybe she'd like to try that again. Next time, I'll be ready for her."

She drew a deep breath, her breasts swelling behind the wrap. "I'm just going to assume that it's the fever talking. You don't look like a stupid man to me, Mister Henry. Only a stupid man would linger in Lone Pine and wait for Renee Stratton to send men for him. Believe me, next time you will not get off so easy!"

"This is easy?" Yakima gave a caustic snort and looked down at his leg. "She branded me for life!"

Beatriz leaned close to him, her large eyes round and

grave. "You didn't listen to me the first time and look what happened! Listen to me now and save your life. I already have two deaths on my conscience. I don't want three."

"I make my own decisions, Miss Salazar. Thanks for the tendin'." Yakima glanced down at his leg. "I'll be takin' my leave from you first thing in the morning."

Her Spanish-dark eyes blazed with quick anger. "Simple fool!"

Again, Yakima took her hand in his. "Whatever happens, it won't be your fault. The kid wasn't your fault, either. Nor mine. What she did to me, I did not deserve, so she's going to have to pay for that. If it kills me."

She drew another deep breath and placed her hand against his face and canted her head to one side. "It will, Yakima. I haven't known you very long, but I feel a tenderness toward you. You rode out there to protect me. You're a good man. If you die by her hand, it will be because of me."

"No." Stubbornly, he shook his head. "Not any more than her husband's death was your fault."

She let her hand slide down his face, frowning.

"You only slept with him. She shot him."

That caused her mouth to open a little with a silent gasp.

Was this the first time it had ever occurred to her that she was not the reason Renee's husband was dead?

A sheen of emotion shone in her eyes.

"Besides," Yakima added, "it wasn't him you were in love with, was it?"

She stared back at him, the skin above the bridge of her nose wrinkling slightly.

Yakima let his hand slide up her arm and across her shoulder to cup her face in his hand again. "It was her."

As she stared back at him, the emotion grew in her eyes.

Suddenly, she lowered her head and sobbed.

***

Two days later, Yakima reined Wolf up to the hitch rack fronting Jack Bowdrie's Guns & Ammo shop on the main street of Lone Pine, near Madame Cavalcanti's tent shack outside of which the turban-clad woman sat stroking her cat. As he swung down from the saddle a girl's voice yelled, "Yakima!"

He turned to see Pearl O'Malley standing on the opposite side of the street, waiting for a log dray to pass and blinking against the dust of the big wagon's churning wheels. When the dray had passed, she jogged to him, stopped before him, and placed her hand on his arm, looking up at him with concern.

"I just heard what happened!" Pearl squeezed his arm

and glanced down at his leg. "Are you all right, Yakima?"

No, he wasn't all right. He'd lain for two days in burning agony in Beatriz Salazar's neat, little brick house in a grove of large cottonwoods at the edge of town, while she tended him with poultices. The pain had seemed to only grow more severe with time. But that was all right. He'd used the pain to propel himself out of bed this morning and to start tending the business he had ahead of him. Business he would not leave this country without finishing. At least, not as long as he was still upright.

The pain was one thing. The indignity of what Renee Stratton had done to him was another thing altogether.

To Pearl, he said, feeling his face warm with humiliation, "I'm fine. A little sore, but I'm fine."

Pearl gazed at him in shock. "I can't...I can't believe she did that to you!"

"I'm fine, Pearl. Run along, now, will you? I have some purchases to make."

Pearl slid her gaze to the sign over the log shop before her and Yakima. "Ammo," she breathed. Returning her gaze to him, she slowly shook her head and said, "Oh, Yakima...don't."

"Like I said, run along, Pearl. I have business to tend." Yakima swung around and stepped up onto the boardwalk fronting the gun and ammo shop. He stopped suddenly, frowning, as a thought came to him. He turned back around to Pearl. "Say...how'd you hear about it?"

"I was just inside the Wooden Nickel," the girl said, canting her head to indicate west along the busy main street. "I was pickin' up a bottle for Pa when I overheard a coupla Bear Track riders braggin' to—"

She stopped abruptly, cupped her hand over her mouth, her eyes widening anxiously.

Yakima turned to peer west along the street obscured with the haze of horse and wagon dust. The Wooden Nickel was a big saloon and gambling parlor a block away, on the opposite side of the street. It had a big red sign over its roofed boardwalk.

Yakima nodded slowly, the heat building in him again. The heat of revenge which he had not realized he would have the opportunity to start exacting so soon. It had been too much to hope for, in fact. His heart fluttered at the prospect.

"Thanks, Pearl." He stepped up onto the boardwalk.

"Yakima, no!" Pearl shrilled behind him.

Ignoring the girl, he went into the shop and closed the door.

He came out a few minutes later, holding six boxes of .44-caliber cartridges for the Yellowboy and his Colt. He walked over to Wolf and deposited all six boxes into a saddlebag pouch then buckled the flap. He looked over Wolf's behind toward the Wooden Nickel obscured by the dust the ore and ranch supply wagons were kicking up in the street.

He'd just untied his reins from the hitchrack when he heard his name called again, this time by a man. He glanced east to see Sarge O'Malley striding toward him in his lumbering, bandy-legged way. Pearl strode beside her father, much fleeter of foot and prettier to look at, though Yakima had hoped he'd seen the last of her today. He should have figured that when he'd come out of the gun and ammo shop and hadn't seen her out here, waiting to pester him some more, that she'd gone to fetch her father, whose five-pointed star flashed in the sunlight now on his lumpy chest as he approached, his expression of concern matching that of his daughter.

Behind them, Yakima saw Madame Cavalcanti staring at him, puffing her opium pipe. Her dark eyes were ridged by ominously furled brows.

"Yakima, I heard what happened," the town marshal said, drawing to a stop before Yakima. "Pearl told me." He shook his head, glowering. "God, I'm sorry. Dirty rotten thing to do to a man—give him a mark like that." He raised an admonishing index finger. "But I did warn you to get the hell out of the country!"

"Couldn't do it. Sic the feds on me, Sarge. I frankly don't care." His reins in his hand, Yakima stepped up beside Wolf then glanced at his old friend once more.

"Just give me a few days, though, will you? I got business to tend before they haul me away."

"Don't do it," O'Malley said. "Don't ride over there. Stay away from the Wooden Nickel, Yakima."

"Please, Yakima," Pearl chimed in. "There's three of them." She glanced at her father, adding, "I saw the Bear Track supply wagon. They must have come to town for supplies."

Yakima stepped up into the saddle and reined Wolf out into the street.

"I know you're good, Yakima," O'Malley said. "You'll likely be able to take them, but if you do, you'll be igniting a powder keg. You won't be able to avoid the blast. Mark my words!"

Those words, however, Yakima just barely heard above the din of the street, for he'd already turned Wolf and was riding west toward the Wooden Nickel.

Chapter 12

Yakima reined up in front of the Wooden Nickel.

A dozen or so horses were tied at the hitchrack. Glancing at the ranch supply wagon also parked in front of the saloon, half filled with feed bags and other supplies, Yakima stepped down from his saddle. He glanced at the batwing doors under the boardwalk awning from which a low hum of conversation and some laughter issued, including occasional female laughter, and pulled his Colt from its holster.

He flipped open the loading gate, plucked a cartridge from his shell belt, and slid the bullet into the single empty chamber, the one beneath the hammer, which he usually left vacant for safety reasons.

He dropped the stag-gripped revolver back into its holster and, leaving the keeper thong over the hammer free, he stepped up onto the boardwalk and pushed through the batwings. He stopped just inside.

He glanced around the half-filled room and spotted them nearly right away. Men who took a hand in doing what the Bear Track people had done to Yakima tended to stand out in a crowd. There might have been twenty of them, but each man's image had been rendered indelible on Yakima's brain.

They stood at the bar that ran along the rear of the room with a big, polished mirror flanking it. They stood a little left of the bar's center. There were three of them, all right. A whore stood with them.

The two on the left were facing the bar. Between them and the third man, on the right, stood the girl. She wore a lacy little black corset, black pantalettes, and she had black feathers in her hair. She stood with her back to the bar, leaning back, her bare elbows on the bar behind her.

The third man stood facing her. He and the girl, a rather plain-faced brunette, seemed to be having a jovial conversation while he ate a sandwich from the free lunch plate on the bar to his right, between him and four men in business suits sipping beers and also partaking of the ham, cheese, crusty brown bread, and pickled eggs.

The girl was speaking with great animation, occasionally throwing her head back and chuckling throatily. As she did, her eyes swept the room, maybe looking for a prospective customer. It was the whore who spotted Yakima first.

Her eyes found him standing just inside the batwings. She began to look away but then, maybe noting the intensity of his gaze, returned her eyes to him and held them there.

She stopped talking and frowned, curious.

The man to her left kept talking to her but then, when he apparently saw that she was distracted, he turned his head to follow her gaze to the source of her distraction.

His eyes held on Yakima, too, and he stopped chewing his mouthful of sandwich.

The girl glanced at him, and her curious frown became more severe.

The man stared at Yakima. Yakima stared back at him, making his expression bland and unreadable though he could not help the intensity and coldness of his jade-eyed stare. The burn of that brand felt nearly as severe as when Renee Stratton had initially pressed the glowing end against his naked flesh. He could feel it burning through his belly and loins.

He could feel it burning all the way to his soul.

The third man blinked for the first time after spotting Yakima. He reached around the whore to tap the shoulder of the man standing just beyond her. Even above the room's conversational din, Yakima heard him say, "Sorenson! Clayton! Check out the batwings!"

Both men turned to him. He jerked his chin toward Yakima. The two others glanced in the back bar mirror then, widening their eyes in recognition, turned full around to face the big man standing in front of the door.

The men and a few working girls occupying tables between the three Bear Track men and the batwings had spied the sudden movement. They turned their own gazes to Yakima. An uneasy current swept through the room as the conversational hum suddenly died, and all eyes shifted between the Bear Track riders and the man most of them probably knew had killed Weldon Stratton.

By ones and twos and then threes and fours, the men and young women sitting in the line of fire abandoned their tables, taking their drinks and their sandwiches and stepping wide or slipping warily past Yakima and leaving the saloon altogether. The whore who'd been talking to the Bear Track rider moved cautiously down the bar to her right, casting nervous glances over her shoulder at Yakima.

The Bear Track man who'd been speaking to her suddenly raised his right arm and pointed an accusing finger at Yakima and said, "You were supposed to get out of the county, breed!"

Yakima didn't say anything. He just stared stonily across the room at his three Bear Track tormentors now standing with their backs to the bar.

The room suddenly fell as quiet as a church on Friday night. The only sounds were the traffic from outside—clomping hooves and turning wheels—and men conversing on the boardwalk, a distant dog's bark...

The three Bear Track men were getting nervous. Yakima could see it in their eyes.

"What the hell do you want?" asked the one on the left. A bead of sweat popped out just below his right eye and rolled into the dark beard stubble on his cheek.

Very quietly and again evenly, Yakima said, "Payment."

The man on the left and the man in the middle glanced at each other quickly, darkly. The man on the right kept his gaze on Yakima. A smile tugged at the mouth of the man on the left, the one who was sweating. He shifted his eyes to the man beside him again—whom Yakima recognized as one of the two men who'd stripped him—and then he returned his gaze to Yakima.

One of the other customers, apparently thinking he wasn't quite as wide of the field of fire as he'd like to be, rose from his chair quickly and, plucking his half-empty beer mug off the table, hurried into the shadows at the room's rear to stand with several other nervous onlookers.

All three Bear Track men slowly slid their right hands toward their holstered revolvers.

Yakima was growing impatient. That impatience was plain in his voice as he suddenly bellowed, "What the hell are you waiting for? *Jerk those smoke wagons!*"

Two did—the man on Yakima's left and the man who'd been talking to the whore.

The man on the left didn't get the barrel of his Remington clear of its holster before Yakima's .44 spoke and punched a bullet through his breastbone. The man on the far right was raising his own Colt, just getting it leveled on Yakima, when Yakima punched his ticket, too—with a round through his neck. The man grunted and fired his own Colt wild as he twisted around, dropping his gun, and thrust his arms across the bar, trying to hold himself up as blood geysered from his neck.

Yakima cocked his Colt again as he slid it a tad to the left, aiming at the man in the middle, who had not reached for his own revolver but left it in its holster. He opened his hands and said, "I didn't pull." His voice was thick and heavy with fear.

"Too bad," Yakima said. "You might have had a chance."

The man's eyes widened, terror glinting in them. "*No!*" he shouted, thrusting his pleading hands toward Yakima, palms out. Yakima's next round blasted a hole through the man's left hand before punching into his left shoulder. The man jerked back against the bar, slapping his right hand to his wounded shoulder.

Yakima fired again. That round punched through the man's right shoulder.

The man wailed and again fell back against the bar.

Yakima's Colt thundered twice more and the Bear Track man who'd stripped off Yakima's pants and long-handles screamed as the bullets smashed into first his left knee and then his right knee and he fell, howling and writhing in misery.

Yakima glanced around the room, half-expecting one of the onlookers to draw a gun and make a fast friend of Renee Stratton. As he did, he emptied his spent shells onto the floor where they clinked and rolled around near his boots and replaced them with fresh from his cartridge belt. Keeping a cautious eye skinned on the onlookers, who appeared satisfied only to slide their shocked gazes between him and the three Bear Track riders, two of whom were dead while the third lay howling and bleeding, Yakima dropped the Colt into its holster and strode forward.

He grabbed the first man he'd shot up off the floor, crouching as he drew him over his right shoulder. He hauled him across the room and outside and flung him into the back of the supply wagon. Still keeping a cautious eye on the still quiet and unmoving crowd, he picked up the second man he'd shot and hauled him out to the freight wagon. He retrieved the wounded rider last and tossed him howling and cursing into the back of the freight wagon with the other two.

When he looked up, Yakima saw Sarge O'Malley and Pearl staring at him from where they stood on the boardwalk fronting the Wooden Nickel. In fact, every person on the street—and there were a good many—had stopped what they'd been doing to stare at him in mute incredulity. Men who'd been riding past the saloon on horseback or in wagons had all stopped to gawk.

"Yakima," Pearl said in a hushed voice, slowly shaking her head in disbelief.

"Good God, man," O'Malley said. "What are you tryin' to do? Bring *hell* down on yourself?"

"I already did."

Yakima untied Wolf from the hitchrack, led the horse around behind the wagon, and tied him to an eye ring on the tailgate.

"I need a doctor!" bellowed the wounded man in the back of the wagon, flopping around on the feed sacks. "Someone fetch me a doctor! I'm hurt *bad!*"

Ignoring him, Yakima climbed into the wagon. He took up the reins, released the brake, then swung the lineback dun in the traces out into the street and then full around, heading west.

"Stop! Damn you, you're *killing me!*" howled the wounded Bear Track rider.

Yakima felt a dark grin tug at his mouth corners as he shook the reins over the dun's back, urging him into a run. The man in the back of the wagon wailed.

When he was half a mile out of town on the road to Bear Track, Yakima stopped the wagon. He tied the reins to the seat then stepped into the back of the wagon and around the two dead men and the wounded man who was bawling now and making strange, coyote-like yipping sounds, like a dying animal.

Yakima reached down over the tailgate to untie his reins from the ring. He pulled Wolf up close to the wagon and stepped over the wagon and onto the black's back.

"Help me!" the wounded rider pleaded, his voice now as high and thin as a girl's.

Yakima pulled his .44 from its holster, cocked the gun, and raised the barrel, aiming skyward. He triggered two shots. The dun whinnied shrilly and went galloping up the trail. It likely knew the way back to the Bear Track headquarters. Horse and wagon and their grim cargo would reach it in under an hour, likely at a fast clip most of the way.

Yakima could see the wounded rider flopping madly around atop the feed bags in the back. He could still hear him screaming.

Again, he smiled.

Quickly, pulling a tan dust cloud along behind it, the horse and wagon and flopping, wailing rider disappeared from view.

Yakima swung Wolf off the trail and booted him into a run.

Time to unleash the war dogs.

Chapter 13

"Hey, boss," said a Bear Track hand named Chavez, one of two Mexicans on the roll, "you best take a look at this!"

McGowan had just led the hands back to the headquarters for lunch after shifting the herds around the Bear Track pastures. Now the foreman slipped his dusty, sweaty mount's saddle cinch and looked over the horse's rump at the short, curly-headed Chavez and two other men sitting their horses outside the corral. "What is it?"

"The supply wagon's comin' in like that dun's got tin cans tied to its tail!"

"What?" McGowan pulled his saddle and blanket off his sweaty, dusty horse and set both on top of the corral. As he did, he peered over the top slat toward the main trail beyond the open gate and the portal.

Sure enough, the supply wagon was rounding the last bend in the trail, just beyond a handful of big cottonwoods; it was beating it toward the headquarters in a full-out run. Now as it approached, McGowan could hear the growing rataplan of the horse's beating hooves and the thunder of the wagon crashing over chuckholes, the sudden violence of which made it fishtail.

"Who in the hell is driving that contraption?" McGowan wanted to know.

He narrowed his eyes as he studied the wagon and the horse racing down the sun-washed trail, heading straight for the open gate and the portal now. The foreman's frown deepened when he saw no one manning the driver's seat.

One of the two other men with Chavez turned to McGowan and said, "Doesn't look like no one's drivin' it, boss!"

McGowan walked out through the corral gate and into the yard just as the dun raced through the portal in a swelter of silver sweat and dust, the wagon sounding like a large pile of lumber tipping over and thundering onto a cobbled railroad platform. The horse slowed in the middle of the yard and then walked, wobbly-footed and blowing hard, over to the water tank at the base of the windmill. It shook its head, making the silver froth fly, then dripped its snout in the tank to draw water.

"Oh-oh," said the third man with Chavez, who, from his perch atop his horse, had a better view inside the wagon than McGowan did.

McGowan walked toward the wagon. "What is it?"

"Bad news, boss," said Chavez as he and the other two mounted men booted their horses over to the wagon.

They got there ahead of the foreman, peered inside, and then turned to McGowan, saying nothing, their brows furrowed, their eyes dark. McGowan stepped up to the wagon and stopped, feeling a sudden hitch in his throat.

"Holy Christ!"

He placed his gloved hands on the wagon's side panel and studied the three men whom he'd sent to town at the crack of dawn for supplies and who had now been carried home lying atop those supplies. Two appeared dead. They were Boyd Hennessey and Jeff Thomas. The third, Ralph Kimball, appeared to still be breathing. At least his chest and belly were rising up and down quickly, and his lips were stretched miserably back from his teeth. He lay on his back and he was groaning and making strangling sounds. That he was in terrible pain there could be no doubt. He appeared to have been shot in both shoulders and both knees.

By now, all of the hands had gathered around the wagon and were gazing silently, incredulously at the carnage inside the box. Footsteps sounded from up at the house, and McGowan stretched his gaze in that direction. Through the limbs of a big pine, he could see Renee's slender figure move out from the front door and across the porch and then down the steps. She came wide of the tree when she stepped into the yard and came walking toward the wagon.

She wore a simple white blouse and a black skirt though nothing looked simple when Renee wore it. She wore high-heeled black boots which kicked up little puffs of dust as she crossed the yard, approaching the wagon and frowning. The men yielded her access to the wagon and she came to within twenty feet. Her gaze found McGowan, and she said, "What's going on? Who drove that wagon into the yard that fast? What—we have another blown horse, now? Probably a broken axle…"

McGowan didn't say anything. Let her see for herself—what she reaped, she sowed…

She stepped up to the wagon and placed her fine, small pale hands on the side panel and slid her gaze into the wagon. With very little expression, her eyes did a brief reconnaissance of the dead or injured men before rising to lock with the foreman's.

She stared at him, her wide, full-lipped mouth contracting as she pursed her lips as though against a bitter taste. "Did these men have enemies, Mister McGowan?"

"Looks that way, boss."

"Who?"

He was flabbergasted by the question. Did she really not know?

"Take a guess, boss." McGowan couldn't keep his peevishness out of his voice even at the risk of a lashing. "Who do you think?"

Her fire red brows furled. "Are you saying you think…"

"Who else? These men had no enemies I know of— leastways none that would send 'em home like this—and I always keep track." McGowan looked around at the other hands standing in stunned silence. "Did they, boys?"

Several shook their heads, another adding, "None that would do this. Whoever did this—he's an awfully sore hombre."

"Maybe in more ways than one," added Chavez with a taut smile.

Renee backed away from the wagon and looked pointedly at her foreman. "Find out! Find out now!"

She turned around haughtily, red hair flying and flashing in the sunlight, and strode, taut-backed, fists clenched at her sides, back to the main lodge.

"We're postponing lunch, boys. Rope fresh horses. I want us on the trail to Lone Pine in ten minutes!"

McGowan started to turn away.

"What about poor ol' Ralph?" someone asked.

McGowan turned back to the wagon. "Oh, hell—I forgot."

He had. His mind was elsewhere, and it, like his guts, was tangled in knots as a voice inside his head regaled him with: *You should have shot him. You should have put a bullet in him right after she branded him, you fool. Sometimes you just can't abide a crazy woman—even when she's Renee Stratton!*

Now he was forced to bring the trouble to town. He didn't like taking Bear Track trouble to town, even with the useless old George O'Malley in charge of the law there.

Sloppy. Damned sloppy!

He glanced around before picking out a red-mustached face set below a butterscotch-colored hat. "Coffee, you an' Kimball are friends, aren't ya?"

Kinch Coffee looked distastefully into the wagon box and nodded.

"You shoot him, then," McGowan said. "There's nothing to be done for him. He's bleeding out fast."

McGowan headed for the corral where some of the other men were already roping mounts in their second strings, dust rising around them and the prancing horses. The foreman's nerves were so tight that he jumped at the sound of the shot.

***

McGowan and the other Bear Track riders galloped into Lone Pine and down its main street less than an hour later, evoking curses from pedestrians and other horseback riders and wagon drivers alike for their reckless ways. Ignoring the complaints, McGowan led his riders at a continued full gallop into the heart of town, reining up in front of the town marshal's office.

Pearl O'Malley sat out front on the small porch, boots crossed on the porch rail before her. Dropping her feet to the floor, the pretty blond blinked and scowled against the dust that had been kicked up by the Bear Track men and waved an irritable hand at it.

"Pearl, where's the marshal?" McGowan asked, also blinking against the dust catching up to him as the rest of his riders pulled up around him.

The girl's slender shoulders rose as she drew a fateful breath. She jerked her head to indicate the closed door to her left.

"Inside. He ain't feelin' all that well."

"Yeah," McGowan said. "Me, neither. Where's the breed?"

"What breed?"

"You know the one. The one who shot my men and hazed 'em back to headquarters in the Bear Track supply wagon. Don't tell me you don't know about it. You know everything that goes on in this town, Pearl."

The girl opened her mouth to reply but stopped when the door latch clicked and the office door swung wide. O'Malley stood on the other side of the threshhold, his clothes disheveled as was the thin, curly hair on his big, balding, hatless head. He held a tin coffee cup but, judging by how glassy his eyes were, McGowan would have bet the seed bull that coffee wasn't in it.

"Good God, man," O'Malley said. "Why'd you let her do it, Garth?"

"You know I didn't have any choice."

"You let her brand him. Why, Garth? You know as well as I do that kid was rotten to the core. If Yakima hadn't given him that pill he couldn't digest, someone else would have sooner or later. Sure as I'm standin' here!"

McGowan frowned. "Yakima?" he canted his head slightly to one side. "How well do you know this man?"

"We were in the army in Arizona together. He's a good man, Garth. He rode out to Bear Track because he wanted to take responsibility for what he did, to tell her how it was. He didn't deserve to be branded, fer chrissakes!"

"Yeah, well...what's done is done." McGowan was surprised to find himself feeling both regretful and guilty. No, the half-breed hadn't deserved to be branded, but he, McGowan, hadn't been man enough to stand up to his boss. He knew what would have happened if he'd kept Renee from doing what she'd intended with that branding iron. He'd have been kicked off the place, his job given to a younger man.

Both jobs—his foreman job and the job he performed

in her bed.

He hadn't wanted to lose either one of those things. But even now, having let her do it, he felt both of those things slipping away from him. Slowly but surely...

"Leave him be," Pearl said, rising from her chair and placing her hands on the porch rail before her. "So you lost three riders. Maybe you deserved to lose them after what you did to him. Call it done."

O'Malley said, "Like Pearl says, Garth, call it done. Leave him be."

"You know I can't do that."

"You need that job that bad? Workin' for *her*?"

McGowan didn't say it, but, yes, he needed it that bad.

"Where is he?" he asked.

"Gone. He left town," Pearl said.

"Which way?"

O'Malley said, "We haven't seen him since he drove your wagon out of town."

McGowan frowned, incredulous. His heart quickened slightly. Feeling a tightness in his throat, he cleared it and said, "Did...did he have his horse with him? When he drove the wagon out of town?"

"He did," Pearl said. "Long gone by now." She shrugged her shoulders and opened and closed her hands on the porch rail.

McGowan's heart quickened again. He hipped

around in his saddle to regard the men behind him then turned back to the marshal and his daughter. "Oh, no he's not! He's heading for Bear Track, an' the only one there is Renee!"

He jerked his horse around. "Come on, boys—we gotta saddle fresh horses and get home!"

He booted his sweaty buckskin into another ground-churning gallop.

His men followed suit behind him, muttering darkly.

As they galloped toward the livery barn, evoking more angry curses, O'Malley and Pearl shared grave looks.

Chapter 14

Yakima put Wolf down the steep slope on the backside of the house, catching glimpses of the big log dwelling through the branches of the Ponderosas standing tall around him. He let the stallion pick his own way around them, riding with a loose hand on the reins.

At the bottom of the slope, he passed through an area roughly fifty yards behind the house where a two-hole privy, a keeper shed, a springhouse, and a woodshed sat—all of log, even the peak-roofed privy. Between these outbuildings lay many apple trees laden with green apples.

Someone here had had a green thumb at one time. Not the woman, surely. To be good with plants, you had to have a soul. She had none. He had understood that when he'd peered into her eyes. No, she had no soul.

As he approached the house's back door which was set up on a ten-by-ten stone stoop to each side of which sat an unpruned raspberry bush, Yakima kept a cautious eye on the windows. He spied no movement. For that he was grateful. He wanted to be in and out of here before the Bear Track riders returned, without complications.

He halted Wolf a few feet from the back door, swung down from the saddle, and dropped the reins. He started toward the door but stopped when footsteps sounded from inside, from just beyond the door. The footsteps grew louder until they stopped, the door latch clicked, and the door squawked open on dry hinges.

She appeared before him, turning sideways and thrusting her arms forward to empty a wash pan into the yard just beyond the stoop, which she had obviously done many times before, for there was a large patch of barren ground there. Just like her heart, her wash water was poison.

When she saw him, her eyes snapped wide, she gave a startled scream, and dropped the pan onto the stoop with a loud clatter and a splash. She swung around and started to run into the house but took only one step before Yakima dove forward and across the stoop, wrapping a brawny arm around her ankles, tripping her. He gritted his teeth against the searing agony the maneuver kicked up in his branded leg.

She screamed again and fell hard.

He gained his feet and dragged her by one ankle across the stoop and into the yard.

"No!" she screamed, rolling onto her back and kicking at him with her other leg. "Let me go, you half-breed son of a bitch!"

He released her only long enough to grab the two ropes he tied loosely around his saddlehorn. As he let go of her ankle, she screamed throatily, "*Help!*" and started to crawl desperately on all fours back toward the open door.

Yakima overtook her easily, grabbed her arm, kicked her onto her belly, and pulled her arms behind her back. He held her wrists with one hand. She fought hard to pull them free, but his grip was stronger than her pull.

On one knee, he tied her wrists together quickly while she screamed, "Help! *Help meeee!*"

"I'm guessin' there might only be a cook an' a hostler on the place, and they're likely out of hearing range or won't get here in time to save you. Not that they could." Yakima picked her up easily and tossed her up onto Wolf's back. "We'll be out of here shortly," he said as he grabbed his reins, swung up behind her, and wrapped one arm around her to hold her in place on the saddle.

She struggled against the ropes to no avail, tossing her head, her red hair flying in his face.

Yakima reined Wolf around and booted him into a gallop, heading back in the direction from which he'd come. As the horse crossed the yard and started up the steep bluff through the pines, she continued to curse and fight the ropes, as angry as a snared catamount.

"What the hell do you think you're doing?" she said when they were halfway up the bluff. "Where are you taking me?"

"You'll see soon enough."

She'd stopped fighting now, apparently surrendering to the tightly knotted hemp. "Are you going to kill me?"

"You'll find out soon enough."

"If you're going to kill me, just kill me and get it over with!"

"Like I said, you'll see soon enough."

She turned her head to gaze back at him over her shoulder. Her gray-tawny eyes were bright with both rage and fear. "What are you planning? You're going to rape me, aren't you? That's it—of course!"

"Don't flatter yourself."

Holding her tightly around the waist, Yakima put Wolf up and over the bluff and into the valley on the other side. After roughly a three-mile ride along the valley to the northeast, a stream curved up to the horse trail he was following, and he put Wolf into the water, which rose to the black's knees. He followed the stream for a mile then left the stream and traversed rocky ground for another quarter mile or so then swung due north.

He was doing his best to cover his tracks.

Renee had stopped talking and sat before him in

sullen silence.

Her body was ridged with fury and trepidation. Remembering the hard, dark, soulless cast to her gaze when she'd pressed the Bear Track brand to his leg, he felt a cold satisfaction in sensing her own fear now. Her fear and helplessness not unlike that which he'd felt a couple of days ago, when she'd sicced her riders on him and they'd held him down while she'd branded him.

He'd ridden through this country before, on his way to Mexico, but was not overly familiar with it. It took him awhile to find the trail he was looking for. When he found the ancient, rutted trace now nearly overgrown with high-desert scrub, he followed it due south and up into bald, stony mountains—a spur of the San Juan Range. He topped a pass and halted Wolf to stare down into the valley on the other side, relieved to see what he'd hoped he'd see—an old ghost town of age-silvered log and mud adobe cabins lined up along the steep, red crag of a ridge rising on his left.

He'd once spent a month here in Sierra Blanca with an old friend, also one he'd known in the army. It was not long after Faith had died, and he'd run into Barney Anders in Saguache, where he'd ridden for supplies. Anders had invited Yakima to spend some time with him here in Sierra Blanca, plundering his mining claim for more of the rich color he'd found roughly a month before. At loose ends and feeling lost and lonely, Yakima had taken the man up on his offer.

Sierra Blanca had been a ghost town even then, several years ago, with only Anders living here with his two mules and a burro, working his claim. Yakima had learned from another, mutual friend who'd worked the claim with Anders after Yakima had that Anders had died when his mine had caved in. The mutual friend had pulled out of Sierra Blanca soon afterwards, so the town should be entirely deserted by now unless someone else had taken over Anders's or any of the other abandoned claims.

Yakima hoped no one had. He wanted to be alone out here—just him and his red-headed tormentor. He didn't see much down there but the derelict cabins and a handful of false-fronted business buildings. The only movement were the tumbleweeds being shepherded amongst the tan-colored rocks and creosote shrubs by the hot desert wind.

"Why did you take me way out here?" Renee said, her voice bitter. "What are you going to do to me?" There was a hopelessness in her voice, as well. She was likely wondering how she'd ever be found out here, a good dozen miles from the ranch.

"Most folks don't venture over those mountains," Yakima said. "On this side, it's all parched desert and rocks. No place for men or cattle."

She glanced over her shoulder at him again. "Why are we here?"

Again, he could hear the fear in her voice, see it in her eyes.

"You'll know soon enough."

She smiled coldly and said, nodding slowly, "Taking your revenge, eh? Get on with it, then, you damned savage. I can take anything you can throw at me!"

"We'll see."

Yakima nudged Wolf on down the slope, following the faint, ancient trace that had once connected Sierra Blanca, however tenuously and distantly, to civilization. As he rode, he kept a wary eye out, scrutinizing the moldering old town, or what was left of it after time's ravages, for occupation. He saw no horse or wagon tracks along the trail, and he thought that was a good indication that no one was around. He saw no other signs of occupation.

The first cabins and falling-down stock pens slid up along both sides of the trail now. None looked recently occupied. A few birds winged in and out of window-less windows and doorless doorways. The cabins gave way to the half-dozen old business buildings, including a three-story, mud brick hotel standing on the street's right side. A badly faded wooden sign stretched across the hotel's third story still announced: EL CAPITAN

HOTEL, but very softly, the letters just barely visible beneath time's fading.

Yakima put Wolf up to one of the two hitchracks fronting the rotting, dust- and tumbleweed-laden boardwalk running along the front of the hotel. The last time he'd been here, The El Capitan had been abandoned but most of its furnishings had remained. It probably would have been too much trouble or too expensive to have the stuff moved elsewhere. Someone must have had high hopes for Sierra Blanca to build such a hotel here, to put so much money into it, and then, after the gold had played out long before anyone had thought it would, to simply walk away from it. As Yakima remembered, the bar had even been stocked, though his friend Barney Anders had been steadily doing his best to unstock it.

Yakima leaped down from Wolf's back then pulled Renee down. She studied him coldly, the warm wind blowing her hair. Such a lovely woman aside from those eyes, which were a devil's eyes. What a shame, he couldn't help thinking. How had she become so sour and brutal? Was it all due to her best friend having slept with her husband and then her, Renee, having shot her husband by mistake?

There had to have been some foundation for her corruption before that.

As Yakima stared down at her, a little color rose in her cheeks.

"What are you looking at?" she snapped, flaring a nostril.

"Nothin'."

He grabbed her arm, nudged her toward the hotel. "It's your lucky day. A fully furnished hotel. Leastways, it was last time I was here."

"Go to hell."

Yakima stepped up onto the boardwalk and opened one of the two large doors that, like the rest of the wood in the town, was as silver as a knife blade. Hinges groaned loudly, echoing around inside the hotel's saloon. Yakima shoved the woman in ahead of him then drew the door closed and looked around.

The saloon looked much as it had the last time he'd been in it. A little more dust, a few more cobwebs hanging from the wagon wheel chandeliers and the game trophies gazing out from where they were mounted on all four walls. The big, impressive mahogany bar with a mirrored back bar ran along the rear of the room. The stairs rising to the upper stories lay to the right—also big and impressive as well as carpeted though the pattern had long since faded.

Yakima moved forward, pulled a dusty chair out from a dusty table. He swept his gloved hand across the seat of the chair, removing some of the dust and mouse droppings. "Take a load off."

"Untie me."

"No."

"There's no reason to keep me tied. You know I'm powerless against you. I'm a small woman. You're a big man."

"Yeah, without your men to back your play, you're not much, are you?"

"Go to hell!"

"Sit down and I'll untie you. You try anything...anything at all..."

She drew a breath, blinked once slowly then stepped forward and eased down into the chair. Yakima pulled his Arkansas toothpick from the sheath on his left hip and used it to saw through the lashings. The rope dropped away, and she pulled her hands in front of her, sucking a breath through her teeth and massaging her chafed wrists.

She looked up at him. "Please tell me what you're going to do with me."

"Nothin' that you expect."

She frowned up at him, curious.

"Stay here," he said. "You're miles from anywhere, and there's wildcats in these rocks. I'm going to stable my horse."

He went out.

She spewed curses at his back.

Chapter 15

By the time they reached headquarters, the Bear Track riders had all but killed their horses. One fell down as soon as it passed through the gate, and the rider leaped free of his stirrup with a yell.

McGowan swung down from his own mount, shucked his Winchester from the boot, and ran up the broad porch steps. He crossed the porch in three long strides, opened the big door quickly, and swung to one side to avoid a possible bullet. When none came, he cocked the rifle, stepped back into the doorway, and aimed the Winchester straight out from his right shoulder.

The near-dark entrance hall before him was empty.

She was gone.

He knew it even before he called her name and only the dungeon-like silence of the house responded.

He turned to regard his men standing around the base

of the porch steps, all wielding Winchesters and looking at him with skeptical frowns on their dusty, sweaty
faces. Their horses stood sway-backed, knock-need, and
sweat-silvered behind them, blowing hard. A few had
found the strength to draw water from the stock trough
at the base of the windmill.

"You men surround the place! Look for tracks!"

McGowan walked into the house.

"Renee!" he called. "Renee—are you here?"

He scoured the place for her, just in case, knowing
the breed wouldn't have kept her here and risked being
confronted by twenty of her riders. He'd taken her elsewhere. To do only God knew what to her...

Brand her?

Probably kill her. Wasn't that what McGowan would
do to anyone with gall enough to do what she'd done to
the breed? Even a woman?

Yeah, he thought he'd probably kill a woman for
doing that to him. For branding him. For forcing him
to wear her mark for the rest of his life right down next
to his privates.

Yeah, he'd kill her. When McGowan found her, if he
ever did find her, he'd find her dead.

McGowan's heart beat like a tom-tom as he moved
back downstairs. He'd taken a quick look into the kitchen
a minute earlier but now he walked farther into it and

saw the rear door standing partway open. Several men were milling just beyond it, muttering.

One called, "Hey, boss—best come take a look at this!"

McGowan crossed the kitchen, stepping around the stout food preparation table, in his mind's eye seeing the old man standing there in his apron, chopping meat for stew. He'd enjoyed cooking a hearty stew, the old man had, while throwing back bourbon and talking with McGowan, who'd sit in a chair in a shadowy corner, smoking and sipping his own glass of whiskey.

The old man was gone, and now she was likely gone, too. *Renee.*

What the hell was going to become now of McGowan himself...?

He shoved the back door open. Three men stood before him, looking down at the wash pan and the wet stone stoop between them and the foreman.

"This is where he grabbed her, then," McGowan said, not enjoying the sound of desperation and urgency he heard in his own voice.

"Hey, boss," another man called from between the woodshed and the privy. He was down on one knee, leaning on his rifle and looking back over his shoulder toward the house. "I have his tracks—he left heading that direction!" He nodded toward the steep, pine-peppered bluff rising at the edge of the yard, fifty yards beyond him.

"Get to the corral!" McGowan yelled. "Rope and saddle fresh horses!"

***

"What the hell do you think you're doing?" Renee said.

Yakima had brought in a fresh poultice that Beatriz had prepared for him. He'd set the poultice on the table Renee was sitting at, in the derelict El Capitan Hotel's saloon, and removed his cartridge belt. Now he unbuttoned the fly of his denims and was rolling them and his summer weight underwear down his legs, wincing at the burn of the branding. He'd had a spare set of duds in his war bag and those were what he was wearing now.

"Nothin' you haven't seen before, lady."

She dipped her chin and flared a nostril at him from where she sat on the opposite side of the table. When he had his pants down to his knees, Yakima sat in the chair and produced the poultice, wrapped in burlap, from a pouch of his saddlebags. Then he withdrew a bottle, also wrapped in burlap, which Beatriz had also provided for cleaning the wound. He removed the burlap from around the poultice then popped the cork on the bottle.

Renee sniffed the air. "She provided the poultice. I'd know that smell anywhere. An old family recipe. How sweet of her to care for her hired killer."

"I thought it was." Yakima lowered the bottle to the grisly, twisted, pink and black burn on his thigh, and poured a goodly portion over it.

He groaned and sucked air through his teeth. "Damn, lady—this really makes me want to draw my gun and put a bullet in your head."

Outside, thunder rumbled distantly.

Yakima turned to gaze out a dirty, fly-specked window. "No, no—don't you rain on me now, dammit!"

Renee frowned. "Why?"

Yakima didn't say anything. He poured a little more whiskey over the burn, set the bottle on the table, and picked up the poultice. He could feel her flinty gaze on him, studying him skeptically.

As Yakima set the poultice on the burn, she narrowed her eyes again, cagily, and said, "You want them to come."

Yakima took a drink from the bottle then reached into the open saddlebag pouch on the table before him. "They'll split up when they lose our sign in the stream. They'll split up and spread out, searching far and wide, in different directions. I'm guessin' one contingent will pick up our sign and follow it over the mountains."

"You're figuring the odds will be more in your favor."

"You got it."

"What if when they pick up our trail, they summon the others and all twenty of my men coming riding in here?" Renee smiled mockingly. "Then what will you do, you dog-eating red man?"

Yakima reached into his saddlebag pouch again and this time pulled out a roll of gauze Beatriz had also provided. "Don't eat dogs."

"What will you do then?"

"Likely die," he said, glancing across the table at her, his gaze as hard and cold as her own. "But I'll be taking you with me."

She tightened her mouth as she stared across the table at him.

He lowered the gauze to his leg and began wrapping it around the poultice.

As he continued to doctor the wound, Renee said, "Can I have some of that whiskey?"

Yakima slid the bottle toward her side of the table. She picked it up and took a swig, swallowed, then took one more. She smacked her lips as she set the bottle back down on the table.

"She provided good whiskey for cleaning that wound."

"How do you know she provided it?"

"Because it has a label on it. Don't tell me you are a labeled bottle drinking red man." Her eyes glittered with sarcasm.

"You're right on both counts." Finished with the gauze, Yakima returned the roll to his saddlebags and cast another cold, dark look across the table at Renee. "You best hope this unlabeled bottle drinking red man doesn't get too deep into that labeled bottle tonight. I've been known to get drunk and tear whole saloons apart single-handed."

She threw her head back and laughed. "Braggart!"

"No tellin' what would be left of a freckled little redhead with a coal black heart."

"No tellin'," she said, mocking his grammar. "Tell me something."

"Anything for you, dear heart." Yakima took another pull from the bottle.

"Are you and she lovers?"

"Beatriz and me?" Yakima smiled and shook his head. "No." He narrowed a curious eye at her. "What makes you ask?"

"I don't know...I thought I sensed an intimacy between you. She seemed so genuinely heartbroken by what I did to you. So angry at me."

No, dear heart, Yakima thought. What you sensed was her intimacy with you.

"She thinks she's responsible."

"She is, partly."

"No, she's not." Yakima took another pull from the bottle then pointed a finger of his hand holding the bottle at her and narrowed one eye in threat. "You're wholly responsible, and I'm going to hold you to account."

"So, you are going to kill me."

"No." Yakima shook his head. "I'm going to go you one step better. I'm going to kill all your men, including your foreman. Then I'm going to ride back to your ranch and burn every goddamn building on the place. When I'm done, there won't be a stick standing."

He took another pull from the bottle and narrowed that threatening eye at her again. "I'm going to ruin you. By the time I'm done, you'll be penniless and working at a brothel in Lone Pine, workin' on your back in your toothless old age. I may remember you for the rest of my days, given what you did to me, but believe me, lady, you'll remember me till the end of yours."

He took another pull from the bottle.

"Go easy on that whiskey," she said.

"Scared?"

She just stared at him across the table, but he liked the fear he saw in those gray-tawny eyes.

Yakima rose, pulled up his pants, buckled his cartridge belt around his waist, and tied the thong to his thigh. He picked up the rifle he'd set on the table then walked stiffly to the door, opened it, and leaned against the frame, staring out. A light rain was falling from a suddenly leaden sky. Distant thunder rumbled.

"Don't you wipe out my trail, damn you," he muttered, reaching into his shirt pocket for his makings sack. "Don't wipe out my sign."

As he built a smoke with his thick, copper fingers, he wondered if he would die here tonight. Then he pondered the fact that he didn't much care either way. One thing he did know, though, was that his threat had not been an idle one. If he were to die, he would damn sure take a few of the Bear Track men as well as its comely owner to hell with him.

He cast a dark look over his shoulder at her.

She stared back at him, her hard eyes reading the threat in his but refusing to yield.

***

When it grew dark, he lit a lamp and, finding enough wood in a shed flanking the hotel, he lit a fire in the stove that sat up near the bar. He cooked a pot of beans and ate it out of the pan with a spoon from his saddlebags. He offered her some, but she said she wasn't hungry and that she hoped he choked on it. She sat alone there at the table near the doors, he at a table near the stove.

The night was quiet. The only sound was the light rain pelting the old building's walls and windows. Briefly, a coyote howled in the far distance and then there was a brief yammering of several coyotes probably picking up the blood scent, then silence.

He finished the beans, scraping the last from the bottom of the pot, then set the pot on the table beside his Yellowboy. He looked over at her. She had her head down, resting on her arms atop the table. He could tell by the slow rasps of her breathing that she was asleep. Her long, curly hair was a flame-red halo about her head.

Yakima yawned as he felt himself growing sleepy despite his gnawing hunger for revenge. He turned the lamp wick halfway down, spreading flickering shadows throughout the room.

He kicked back in his chair, crossed his legs at his ankles on the edge of the table, set the Yellowboy across his thighs, one hand curled around the neck, the other around the forestock, and closed his eyes. Sleep came lightly, the kind he'd cultivated over the years—a sort of half-consciousness in which he could still sense any doings around him.

He could hear the woman breathing softly and slowly, and he could hear the rain, the slight stirring of a breeze making the old walls creak around him. The scratching of a mouse somewhere behind the bar...

The faint rattle of a bridle chain.

He opened his eyes and lifted his head.

Chapter 16

Yakima looked over at the woman.

He could see only her outline in the darkness. The rain had stopped. The moon had come out, slanting a milky shaft through a dirty window and across her head, casting her red hair with a silvery sheen.

She was still asleep. He could hear her slow, steady breaths.

He rose silently with the Winchester, set his hat on his head, and walked lightly, on the balls of his feet, into a storage room behind the bar. He crossed to a rear door and stood with his head bowed, listening. Hearing nothing, he opened the door very slowly, wincing at the ratcheting sounds of the dry hinges then poked his head out and looked around.

The moon cast a ghostly pearl light, silhouetting the abandoned buildings and the mountain sage against it, slanting shadows along the ground. Nothing moved.

Yakima drew the door closed then swung to his left and walked along the rear of the hotel. He stopped at the far corner, doffed his hat, and edged a look up along the side of the building to the front.

Spying no movement, he turned to his right and walked straight out away from the hotel, keeping it between himself and the main street in front of the place. He walked around behind the stable and several other slouching outbuildings including a roofless stock pen, then swung left and walked a couple of dozen yards, crouching, holding the Yellowboy down against his right leg so the moonlight would not glint off of it, then turned left again. He strode through an alley between two more tall business buildings, heading for the main street.

When he reached it, he edged another look around the corner of the building on his left, staring back toward the hotel which was two buildings away from him now. Shadows moved in front of the hotel. The darkness of the building hid the figures from the moonlight, so Yakima could see only uncertain dark shapes against the dark velvet of the hotel's front wall.

However, on the other side of the street and maybe fifty yards beyond the El Capitan, moonlight pooled on the backs of four horses tied to a hitchrack.

There were four men here, not twenty. Which meant

Yakima had guessed right—they'd split up so they could cover more ground faster.

He felt the corners of his mouth quirk slightly in satisfaction.

He stepped around the corner of his covering building and made his way quietly along the boardwalk fronting the place, heading toward the hotel. He held the Yellowboy down low against his leg but was ready to bring it up fast.

The night was so quiet, he heard one man whisper to the others, though he couldn't make out what was said. Another man grunted as though in acknowledgement.

There were the loud, metallic ratcheting of four rifles being cocked and the pounding of boots on the board-walk. The shadows jostled then merged, disappearing into the greater shadow of the hotel as they pushed through the door.

One of the men yelled suddenly, "Mrs. Stratton—you here?"

In his mind's eye, Yakima watched her jerk her head up suddenly in the near-dark saloon.

"I'm here! Polk, is that you?"

Yakima quickened his pace, broke into a jog.

From inside the hotel, Polk said, "Yeah, it's me and McGraw, Tabor an' Bill Blackwell. Where's he at, Mrs. Stratton? Where the hell is he?"

***

Renee looked around quickly, the blood rushing through her veins.

She returned her gaze to the four men clad in yellow rainslickers standing before her and to her right, in front of the batwings twenty feet away. Each one held a cocked Winchester to his shoulder and, crouched, with boots spread a little more than shoulder-width apart, slid the rifles around, trying to pick out a target.

Renee leaped to her feet, heart pounding. "I don't know—he was here…he was over…"

She let her voice trail off, for she'd just returned her gaze to the four Bear Track men standing before her, cheeks snugged up to the rear stocks of their rifles, their eyes wide and anxious, glinting in the light of the low lamp and the moonlight. A shadow moved behind them, straight out beyond the batwings.

Renee's heart leaped into her throat and she screamed, "Behind you! He's *behind* you!"

They wheeled, each man spinning on one foot. Before they could get their rifles leveled again, the batwings burst inward as bullets ripped through them and into the Bear Track riders—one bullet after another, the sudden fusillade almost sounding like one long shot. Between each quick, ripping report, Renee heard the metallic rasp of the half-breed's rifle being cocked, sending another round into the action...another round into another of her four would-be rescuers.

She looked on in mute astonishment as one by one, the four men were punched backward, twisting around and doing ridiculous-looking pirouettes, one firing his rifle into the ceiling then screaming shrilly as another bullet punched into him and he tossed his rifle onto a table then fell in a heap and rolled up against a leg of the table Renee stood at.

Her lower jaw hung.

The big half-breed moved forward, his broad-shoul-dered silhouette growing larger as he stepped through the bullet-shredded batwings. He stepped into the flick-ering lamplight, his jade eyes darting from one dead man to another.

Only, one wasn't dead. Lying belly down on the floor directly in front of the batwings, Bill Blackwell moved his hatless, nearly bald head and said through a toneless groan, "Don't...don't...kill..."

The half-breed's rifle drowned Blackwell's last word.

The man's head jerked violently, and then he lay still.

***

Yakima turned to the woman. She stood staring at him,

her face expressionless though her mouth was halfway open. He extended his hand to her. "Come on. We're goin'."

"Go to hell."

Yakima walked over and grabbed her by the back of her neck and shoved her out through the ruined batwings, one of which hung by only one hinge. He hazed her down the side of the building to the stable, opening the stable door and shoving her inside then closing the door behind her. He had to keep her away from the guns of the four men he'd just killed.

He lit a lamp, hung it from a ceiling support post and turned to find her edging stealthily back toward the door.

"You stay here where I can see you or I'm gonna knock you out with my rifle butt and tie you belly down across the saddle."

She drew a breath, pressed her back against the closed stable door, and crossed her arms on her chest. Her face was stony but her shoulders trembled.

Quickly, keeping one eye skinned on the woman, Yakima saddled Wolf. He led Wolf and the woman out of the stable and over to the four horses standing tied to the hitchrack up the street and to the north of the hotel. Quickly, he untied a lean blue roan from the hitch rack then flung her up into the saddle so quickly she gave a shrill little scream, lunging for the horn.

Wheeling, Yakima swung up onto Wolf's back and,

leading Renee's horse by its bridle reins, ground his heels into Wolf's flanks, pounding up the trail in the opposite direction of the pass. He galloped to the edge of town and into the moonlit desert beyond it, putting Sierra Blanca behind him likely for the last time.

They hadn't ridden far when she yelled behind him, "I'm cold! It's cold and damp!"

Yakima reined in, curveted Wolf and looked back at her.

She wore only the blouse and skirt she'd been wearing when he'd first nabbed her earlier that day. Yakima swung down from Wolf's back and untied his bedroll. He'd rolled his denim jacket in it as well as the four-point capote he wore in the winter—if he didn't make it to Mexico, that was. He usually tried to make it to Mexico but a couple of times he'd been unlucky enough to get caught in Dakota Territory for the winter though, despite a good woman he'd met up there on one of those trips, he'd vowed to never let that happen again.

He held both garments up for Renee to scrutinize.

"Which one do you want?"

"The light jacket will do."

Yakima tossed it to her then rolled his coat in the blankets and strapped the roll to his saddle again, behind the cantle. He mounted up, said, "Hold on tight, now," and booted Wolf on ahead.

He paused a couple of times to cover his tracks then,

near dawn, spied a canyon that appeared a good, well-concealed place to camp. He rode down, leading the woman's horse then rode along the canyon floor from which the night's shadows lifted as the dawn grew. He found a cave in the base of the canyon's southern wall. After a brief inspection, finding only some old rabbit bones inside but nothing to indicate the cave was still home to a painter or other deadly prey, he stripped the tack from both horses and set up camp in the cave.

Renee didn't help.

She just sat on her butt against a cave wall, knees drawn up to her chest, staring at him in that cold, stony silence he'd come to know so well.

He found some relatively dry wood and brush, built a stone fire ring, and set to work building a small fire for coffee. He made the mistake of turning his back on her to coax the flames to life by blowing on them. Her shadow slid along the cave floor beside him. He'd just started to turn when he felt the hard blow of what could only have been a rock smashed across the crown of his head.

"Ah, hell," he heard himself grunt, blinking his eyes, trying in vain to clear them.

The cave pitched around him like a small boat in choppy seas. He sagged to one side, thrust his left hand down to keep himself from falling. A cold worm turned in his belly when he heard the snick of his Colt leaving the holster on his right thigh.

Another cold worm turned inside him when he heard the click of the hammer being cocked. Adrenaline flooded him and before he knew what he was doing, he rolled onto his side, saying, "Oh, no you don't!" and kicked her feet out from under her.

She screamed and the gun roared, smashing the bullet into the cave floor just inches to the left of Yakima's head. She fell hard with a resolute thud. Still fighting to stay conscious, feeling as though his head were a cracked egg, Yakima grabbed his gun out of her hand.

She lay on her back, groaning and blinking, pressing the heels of her hands to her temples.

Yakima sat back against the cave wall, shaking his head, trying to clear the cobwebs. He reached up to probe the back of his head with his fingers. They came away sticky with blood. He could already feel the beginnings of a goose egg up there. He'd have a sizeable one.

He started to rake out a curse but stopped when he heard the distant thuds of galloping horses. Then a man's voice, also distantly but clearly, said, "It came from down there!"

Renee must have heard it, too. She sat up quickly, her eyes wide and desperate as she turned her head toward the cave opening and screamed, "McGowan, I'm here! *I'm down here!*"

Chapter 17

Yakima lunged for the woman, closed a hand over her mouth and shoved her back down onto the cave floor. He ripped off his neckerchief and tied it over her mouth. He reached for his lariat then rolled her onto her belly and used the lariat to hogtie her.

Gaining his feet heavily, still weak and dizzy from the braining she'd given him, he grabbed his hat, which she'd knocked off his head, and reshaped and donned it. He grabbed the Yellowboy, stepped out of the cave, and peered up the ridge.

A large mare's tail of dust shone above the ridge, trailing off to the east, to Yakima's right. The riders were looking for a way into the canyon.

Yakima cursed. He wasn't ready for them. Not with his aching head and his vision cloudy. But they were coming, anyway.

He glanced back into the cave. Renee lay belly down, trussed up like a calf for the branding. She grunted behind the gag, glaring at him, her face flushed with rage. He could read what her eyes were telling him, promising him.

"Now, you're going to die bloody, red man! Now you'll die bloody!"

If so, it was his own damn fault.

He pumped a round into the Winchester's action and stepped around the two horses he'd tied to a gnarled cedar. In passing, he absently patted Wolf's left hip. "Stay, boy. You stay. Gonna do this alone."

He stepped out onto the canyon floor and, suppressing the misery in his head, he jogged back in the direction that he and Renee had come. He'd walked maybe a hundred yards when he spied movement on the ridge ahead of him. The riders had followed the curve of the canyon to the far end and had found the trail down the ridge. They were just now taking it, first the lead rider then another and another until five horseback riders were dropping down the ridge at a slant from Yakima's left to his right, the tails of their horses arched.

Yakima looked around quickly. It was five against one. He needed high ground.

His eyes found a rocky escarpment jutting on his right and tufted with sage and cedars. He followed a crease between boulders and walked around the side of the escarpment, looking for a way up. Finding a route with plenty of shelving rocks, clefts and fissures, he took the Yellowboy in one hand and started climbing, using the rocks and the brush for handholds. As he climbed, he kept a sharp eye out for rattlesnakes. He didn't need a snakebite to add misery to his agony.

It was hot and he was sweating through his shirt by the time he'd gained the escarpment's crest. He rose from his knees then quickly dropped low again when he saw the dust of the oncoming riders ahead of him, maybe a quarter mile away and moving closer. He dropped to his belly and crawled forward along the relatively flat top of the escarpment, heading back in the direction of the riders.

As he crawled, the thudding of the horses rose. It grew quickly louder until Yakima could hear the squawk of tack and the rattle of bridle chains, as well. Two men were talking quietly, in hushed tones, before one said loudly enough for Yakima to pick up, "Keep a sharp eye out, fellas. Keep a sharp eye out!"

Yakima, who had gained the edge of the scarp, snaked his Winchester over the side, aiming at a downward slant, and said, "Too late."

He lined up his sights on the first rider—the big, mustached foreman, McGowan, who had just snapped his startled gaze up to Yakima—and pulled the trigger.

The man's horse whinnied and reared sharply. The big foreman went tumbling down the Appaloosa's right hip with an indignant wail, losing his hat as well as the rifle he'd been holding across the pommel of his saddle.

Yakima ejected the smoking cartridge and seated a fresh one, lining up his sights on the second man in the pack who was just then bringing up his own rifle. Yakima fired and watched in grim satisfaction as the bullet punched through the man's chest and sent him rolling backward over the tail of his horse. As he piled up on the trail, he was kicked in the head as the horse of the rider behind him spun fearfully, whinnying shrilly.

"Ambush—spread out!" shouted one of the three others, who were just then leaping from their saddles and scattering into the rocks and brush along both sides of the trail.

Yakima fired again and cursed when his bullet merely plumed dirt and gravel several inches behind the man who'd just then dove behind a rock to his right. He racked another round and pulled his head down as a rifle poked out from behind a small boulder resembling a table with only two legs, and the eye of the man wielding it narrowed to line up the sights on him.

The rifle crashed, and the bullet sang through the air where his head had been an eye blink before.

Yakima lifted his head and raised his rifle but the man who'd just fired had pulled his own head back behind the boulder. Catching a glimpse of another rifle bristling at him from between a large, pale rock and a juniper, he pulled his head down again just in time to keep from getting drilled a third eye. He turned his body sideways atop the scarp and rolled away from the edge.

When he thought he was out of view from below, he rose and ran back along the escarpment, heading for its backside. He didn't want to get trapped up here and find himself firing off all of his rounds. He wished he would have brought one of the boxes he'd bought in town. As it was, he had only those remaining in the Winchester and in the leather loops of his cartridge belt.

He had to get this finished fast—not only because he was short on ammo, but because the others, possibly having heard the rifle fire, might be on their way.

He stopped at the back of the escarpment and edged a look down the other side. All clear. His stalkers hadn't worked around him. At least, not yet.

Spying a way down, he sank to his butt and dropped his legs over the edge then turned to face the escarpment. He'd just started clambering down when he saw something move in a crenelation in the scarp to his left. His guts turned to ice when he saw the flat, diamond-shaped head and eerie, colorless eyes of the snake poking its head out of the crack—the same crack he'd just grabbed the edge of with his left hand.

"Oh!" He pulled his hand away but not before feeling the snake's head graze the side of it as it struck.

Shit!

Yakima leaped to a two-foot-wide shelf of rock five feet below him then, still feeling the chill of the near-bite in his loins, he quickly clambered the rest of the way to the ground, leaping the last several feet. Facing the scarp, he looked to his left and then to his right and instantly dropped belly down.

The man he'd just seen aiming a rifle at him—a beefy fellow with a shaggy beard who Yakima recognized as the son of Satan who'd ripped off his shirt and sat on his chest while Renee had branded him—cut loose with his Henry repeater. The Henry's octagonal barrel roiled orange flames and pale smoke. Yakima stuck his Winchester out in front of him, slid his cheek up against the rear stock, aimed, and fired.

Another damn miss as the bearded bastard stepped behind a boulder.

Yakima gained his feet and, ejecting the smoking cartridge and hearing it clink onto the rocky ground behind him, he pumped a live one into the action. He ran forward, heading for the boulder behind which his bearded tormentor had just taken cover. He was within ten feet when the man poked his head and Henry out from behind it, aiming at Yakima.

Yakima stopped and, just ahead of the Henry's roar, threw himself to his right, yelping at the misery the maneuver kicked up in his branded leg. He rolled once to his right, aimed at the bearded man, and fired.

The man was just then pulling his head behind the boulder, but Yakima's slug smashed into the corner of the boulder, near the man's left eye, and pelted the man's face with rock shards. The man yelped and disappeared behind the rock.

Yakima heaved himself to his feet and ran forward once more. He gained the rear of the boulder and stopped, aiming his rifle into the gap between it and another one behind it. The bearded man was stumbling away from Yakima, cursing loudly, holding his rifle in one hand, holding his other hand to his face. He had his back to Yakima but, apparently sensing the man behind him, he stopped and swung around.

He held one large fat hand over his left eye. Blood oozed out from behind it.

"Bastard!" he wailed and started to bring the Henry up again.

He didn't get it half-raised before Yakima's Yellowboy spoke twice, neatly placing two puckered, blue, 44-caliber-sized holes in his forehead, roughly six inches apart. The man's head jerked back savagely. He followed it with his feet, heavy-footed, and fell in a quivering heap.

Spying a sun reflection to his left, Yakima stepped forward, behind the boulder.

A rifle roared. Yakima wheeled and edged a look out from behind the boulder. Two rifles were aimed at him—one from behind a wagon-sized boulder ahead on his left, the other from behind a wheelbarrow-sized chunk of granite on his right.

Yakima pulled his head back as the rifle ahead and on his left thundered. The bullet smashed into nearly the same place that his own had when it had made the bearded man one-eyed for the brief remainder of his allotment. Plucking fresh rounds through the Yellowboy's loading gate, Yakima jogged along the backside of the boulder, leaping the dead, bearded, one-eyed gent. He ran out from behind the boulder, swung left, and kept running. When he gained the opposite side of the boulder from where he'd killed One-Eye, he stepped out around it and aimed the Winchester straight out from his right hip.

Sure enough, the last two Bear Track men were straight out ahead of him now, in profile, fifty feet away. He could clearly see both men covering behind their respective rocks. They were aiming their rifles at where Yakima had been two minutes ago.

Yakima gave a low whistle.

Both men jerked astonished gazes at him, swinging their rifles around, as well.

Yakima shot the nearest man, the one behind the wheelbarrow-sized chunk of granite, first. He cocked and fired at the farthest man second, but his target twisted to one side and the round merely clipped his check-sleeved left arm. He spun around, cursed, and ran behind the big escarpment from which Yakima had first fired on these sorry sacks of burning dog dung.

Yakima ran forward and around the escarpment and back in the direction from which he'd descended it. He glimpsed the last Bear Track rider—a thick-set man in a brown shirt and a black vest and black hat—swinging left and disappearing into a gap between two boulders. Yakima followed him, running hard and gritting his teeth against the burning pain in his branded thigh.

He'd last seen the man he was chasing on the horse that had dragged him to the branding fire. He'd recognize that back and red neck anywhere.

He stepped into the gap and stopped, aiming the Winchester out from his right hip, index finger drawn taut against the trigger, ready to fire. But his quarry was not before him. Slowly, Yakima moved forward, ready for the man to appear suddenly, rifle aimed...

He'd taken a half-dozen steps when gravel crunched softly behind him. The man had worked around him!

A hammer pinged benignly.

Yakima wheeled and fired but as he did his right

boot came down awkwardly on a rock, and his bullet merely cut a red line across the outside of the left cheek of the man before him. The man, having found his rifle empty, gave an enraged wail as he lunged forward, raising the rifle like a club. Yakima had just lowered the Yellowboy's cocking lever to seat another round into the action when the man smashed his own Winchester into the Yellowboy, knocking it out of Yakima's hands then bulling himself into Yakima, head-butting him then driving him to the ground.

"Dirty, murderin' devil!" the man wailed, sitting up as he straddled Yakima and raised his right arm and clenched right fist.

He was big and he was strong, but Yakima thrust up his left arm and managed to deflect the blow of the man's large fist. Then he smashed his own right fist into the man's face once, twice, three times—solid, brain-jarring blows that drove the man back and to one side, his nose and his lips bloody.

Yakima pushed to his feet, bells still ringing in his head from the head butt so close on the heels of Renee's blow. Shaking his own head as though to clear it, his opponent rose, as well. Yakima crouched, boots spread, clenching his fists, and the two men traced a slow circle, glaring at each other like two proud bulls in the Texas Big Thicket.

"How'd you like that draggin', you red devil?" the

man growled, smiling coldly, showing his large, to-bacco-stained teeth beneath his red mustache. "Did that feel good?"

Yakima lunged forward in a blur of quick motion and, furiously clenching his teeth, delivered a powerful right jab to the man's mouth, further opening his lips so that blood ran in two streams down over his chin.

That incensed his opponent. "Why, you—!" The man lunged forward, intending to deliver an uppercut to Yaki-ma's jaw. The dull-witted ape telegraphed the move with his eyes, and Yakima was ready for him, pulling his head back and to one side so that the man's knuckles delivered a mere glancing blow to his left cheek then stumbled forward, propelled by his own momentum.

He stumbled forward and into Yakima's right fist again.

Smack! Smack! Smack!

Yakima delivered the jabs with both fists and without mercy.

The man grunted with each blow and, astonishment widening his eyes, he staggered backward. Then rage darkened his gaze again and he slid his right hand to the Colt holstered on that thigh.

Yakima took two quick steps forward and kicked the gun out of the man's hand then delivered to his face, which already looked like ground burger, three more smashing blows. He followed that up with a powerful roundhouse that sent the man to the ground in a pile.

He lay on his side, bleeding and groaning, slowly shaking his head.

Yakima walked over and picked up the Yellowboy. He brushed sand and gravel from it and finished cocking it.

The big man opened his eyes, gazed up fearfully at Yakima. Again, he shook his head. "Don't...don't... kill me."

"You were dead the day you dragged me to that branding fire."

Yakima drilled a round between the man's eyes.

The thuds of a running horse rose from the direction of the trail.

Yakima swung around and ran through the rocks and boulders, wending his way back toward the trail while replacing the spent brass in his Winchester. He was a hundred feet from the trail when the rider passed before him, galloping like a bat out of hell from Yakima's left to his right. The man was big, and he was crouched low in the saddle, cupping his right hand to his bloody left shoulder.

Yakima got only a brief glimpse of him before he disappeared on down the trail. But with that brief glimpse, he'd recognized him.

McGowan.

Yakima must have only wounded the man.

PETER BRANDVOLD

He increased his pace and when he gained the trail, he wheeled to face the direction the foreman had gone. He raised the Winchester and aimed straight out from his right shoulder then lowered it, cursing.

The man had just disappeared around a bend in the trail, the thuds of his horse dwindling quickly.

190

Chapter 18

It was quiet in the bank, with only one customer doing business at one of the teller cages, so Beatriz poured herself a cup of coffee from the pot she always kept warming on the stove in a corner of the lobby. It was a holdover custom from her father. He'd always made coffee available for staff as well as for customers. And for himself, as well. A big coffee drinker had been Diego Salazar.

Beatriz smiled now, remembering the garrulous man fondly, and missing him. Without him here in the bank with her and without him in the house she'd grown up in, she felt very much alone. Thinking of her loneliness turned her thoughts to Renee, and then, as though that thought had conjured it, a man's voice on the street shouted, "Hey, McGowan—what happened to *you?*"

Beatriz had been walking back to her office, holding the warm stone mug in both hands, but now she stopped and turned to face the big, plate-glass window that looked out onto the street. The street was bustling with horseback riders and wagon traffic, but her gaze quickly picked out the large, raw-boned, dark-mustached man just then riding past the bank on a sweaty Appaloosa, heading from Beatriz's right to her left. McGowan rode crouched low in his saddle, holding his right hand against his right bloody left shoulder.

As he was about ride on past the bank, the Bear Track foreman glanced over his shoulder and yelled, "Cut myself shavin'!" Then he turned his head forward again and rode on past the bank and out of Beatriz's view.

In that brief glance at the man's rugged face, she had seen the hard set to his features. He was in pain.

Dread touched Beatriz. She found herself moving slowly forward, walking toward the window then turning her head to peer down the street on her left, following the big Bear Track foreman with her gaze. She was not surprised to see him angling toward the office of Dr. Luis Dragoman—a white-frame clapboard building sitting between a barber shop and the Lone Pine Opera House on the opposite side of the street from the bank.

Dread building in her, Beatriz set her coffee down on the small table by the stove, strode quickly to the bank's front door, and went out. She walked down the boardwalk in the direction of the doctor's office, lifting her skirts above her ankles, quickening her pace. As she started to cross the street, she saw McGowan climb heavily down from the Appaloosa's back. Beatriz increased her pace to avoid an oncoming lumber dray, and as she approached the foreman, who was walking heavily toward the hitch rack in front of his horse, she said, "McGowan, what's happened?"

The foreman tossed his reins over the hitchrack and turned to her, his eyes bright with pain, the deeply tanned skin drawn taut over the hard plains of his face. "Your Injun took her."

"What?" Beatriz slapped her hand to her chest. "Who?" But she knew. Still, she had to hear it.

"Who do you think? Renee. He took her. He's using her as bait. He's tryin' to kill every damn one of us, and he's gettin' close!" McGowan swung around uncertainly, as though drunk, and tripped and nearly fell climbing up onto the boardwalk fronting the doctor's office.

"Where are they?" Beatriz asked, her heart hammering.

Again, McGowan turned his pain-bright gaze to her. "Other side of Dead Horse ridge, holin' up in them rocks over there." He started to turn away but then turned back to her and spit out bitterly, "You really should've kept him on his leash, lady. If he gets the rest of the hands, you can bet he's gonna kill her, too!"

Rage rose in Beatriz. She clenched her fists at her

sides as she bent forward and yelled, "You make it sound as though it's my fault! You let her brand him! What did you think would happen?"

He gave a caustic laugh, stretching his lips away from his teeth. "Oh, I knew!" He laughed again and then staggered toward the door, saying as he grabbed the knob, "Oh, I knew! Shoulda put a bullet in 'im, but you know as well as I do there's no reasoning with Renee!"

He fumbled the door open, stumbled inside, and closed the door behind him.

Beatriz stood staring at the door in shock.

He took her. He's usin' her for bait...

"My God," she heard herself mutter, still staring at the glass-paned door of the doctor's office. "My God..."

She'd feared something like this. She'd managed to, for the most part, put the whole mess out of her mind for the past two days. She'd decided to release her worry because there was nothing she could do. The situation was out of her hands. She supposed she'd resigned herself to the fact that Yakima would seek the revenge he so desperately wanted—and what man wouldn't want revenge for what she'd done to him?— and that he'd likely die seeking it.

He was only one man. He was up against too many.

But he'd found a way...

Renee.

Beatriz turned and suddenly found herself walking

in the direction of the livery barn. She needed a horse. Her own horse was only a puller. She needed a horse she could ride.

"Mister Flynn, I need a horse. A fast horse," she told the liveryman a few minutes later. "I would also like him delivered to my house within the half hour, please. Leave him at the fence."

A middle-aged man in bib-front overalls and with untrimmed gray hair and gray mustache, Flynn was standing outside his sprawling livery barn, smoking a loosely rolled cigarette. He glanced skeptically at the west-edging sun and said, "Kinda late in the day for a ride—ain't it, Miss Salazar?"

She turned and headed back in the direction from which she'd come, saying curtly over her shoulder, "Within the half hour, please, Mr. Flynn."

***

"How many have you killed so far?" Renee asked. "Are you carving notches on your pistol butt?"

She sat across the small fire Yakima had built to make coffee and heat some beans, which they'd eaten. Now they each sat with a cup of coffee. Yakima was keeping her tied now after she'd brained him, but he'd released her hands for the time being so she could eat and drink coffee. He'd kept her ankles bound, however. And he was making damn sure not to turn his back on her.

Fool me once, shame on you...

They'd left the canyon right after Yakima had watched McGowan ride out with a bullet in his shoulder. They were several miles from the chasm in which he'd left four more Bear Track men dead, back on the other side of the mountains and on Bear Track land. Since Yakima had winnowed down the Bear Track payroll considerably, he didn't want to make it too hard for the rest to find him.

Little by little, he'd been accomplishing his mission.

"Funny, I was just wondering that myself." Yakima sat back against his saddle and sipped the coffee he'd just replenished. "Let me see..." He lifted his head and scratched his chin. "With the first three in town, the five in Sierra Blanca, and the four I left in the canyon—I do believe twelve." He smiled across the fire at her.

"I'm surprised you can count that high."

"Don't be. Hell, I even taught myself to read. Not much of a book-readin' man, but I can read a newspaper and sign my name."

Renee sipped her coffee. "You're good at killing, too. I have to say I'm impressed." She looked down into her cup and smiled, shook her head. "I should've listened to my foreman." She drew her mouth corners down and shook her head again. Then she looked across the fire at him once more. "The odds are still against you, though. With McGowan, I still have eight men left."

"McGowan's packin' lead. Prob'ly out of commission for a while."

She stared darkly across the fire at him, considering that. Frowning, suddenly, she said, "Is this making up for it? What I did to you."

"Go on—you can say it. You branded me. Marked me for life. And to answer your question, yes."

But was it really? Not, not really. But what choice did he have? When someone did to him what this woman and her men had done to him, they had to pay the price. If not, they'd only be emboldened to try it again. To someone not as handy at exacting comeuppances.

She sipped her coffee, kept it in her mouth, and nodded before swallowing. "I can understand. I suppose I would want the same. Any of my men would want the same. Rather savage rules we live by, aren't they?" She smiled as though impressed at the notion.

"They are," Yakima agreed.

She swirled the coffee in her cup, staring down at it, then cast that gray-tawny gaze across the fire at him again. "If your luck holds and you do manage to kill every man who was at the headquarters that day, and you burn me out, I'll never forget it." She smiled and shook her head. "Never in a million years."

"Like you said, lady," Yakima said, tossing another small branch on the fire, "savage rules we live by." He set his cup down and climbed to his feet. "Now, if you'll excuse me..."

He grabbed his rifle, not wanting to leave it anywhere near his captive when her hands were free and started walking into the brush beyond from the fire.

"I need to take that walk soon, too," she called after him.

"We'll see."

Yakima had just stopped walking and had started to unbutton his fly when he froze. He'd heard something.

"What was that?" Renee called.

"Listen."

It came again—a hoof thud.

Yakima swung around and ran back into the camp. He was about to kick dirt on the fire when a woman's voice rose from the darkness: "Yakima?"

He forestalled the kick and stared off into the night lit by a high-kiting three-quarter moon. The voice had been lightly Spanish accented. Yakima frowned. "Beatriz?"

"I'm riding in."

"Well, well," Renee said, curling a devilish smile at him. "Your woman couldn't stay away from you."

What if it were you she came to see? he felt like asking her but did not.

The hoof thuds grew louder until the fire was reflected in the eyes of the approaching horse and then in its rider's. Beatriz rode in wearing black denims and a heavy brown cape with a hood. She stopped the horse before Yakima.

"What the hell are you doing out here?" Yakima asked her, casting his gaze into the moon-dappled forest behind her and sliding his right hand to his Colt. "Were you followed?"

Beatriz lowered the hood, shook her head, and her thick, dark hair danced across her shoulders. "I made sure. I wouldn't lead them to you." Her eyes were dark and grave as they slid to Renee.

Renee crooked that devious smile at her and said, "Couldn't stay away from him, eh?"

Beatriz shook her head. "We're not lovers, Renee."

"Why not?" Renee glanced at Yakima. "A good-lookin' devil for a red man. For a kill-crazy half-breed son of a bitch. I bet he'd love to curl your toes for you, Beatriz. We both know how much you enjoy having your toes curled. Or maybe you wouldn't consider him since he's not married."

"Please, don't talk like that, Renee. That's not who you were once."

"It's who I am now."

Yakima stepped forward and looked down at Beatriz. "What are you doing out here?"

"I rode out to look for you. It's crazy, I know. I was going to ride over the spur ridge. That's where Mc-Gowan said he'd last seen you. But then I saw a fire, hoped it was you."

"It could have been her men." Yakima canted his head at his hostage.

"But it wasn't."

Yakima shook his head, scowling. "I don't understand."

"I had to see you." She turned to Renee. "I had to see my old friend, Renee. McGowan said you'd taken her. That you were killing his men…" She turned back to Yakima. "Do you intend to kill her, too?"

"What's it to you?" Renee asked.

Beatriz kept her brooding, dark gaze on Yakima. "Do you?"

Yakima shook his head. "Just her men. I'm going to leave her with nothing."

Beatriz turned to Renee and nodded slowly, pondering. "I see."

Renee said, "You'd rather he killed me, wouldn't you?"

Beatriz swung down from the saddle, absently cradled her horse's head in her arm and ran her other hand affectionately, absently down its snout. "Why would you think such a thing?"

"You would, wouldn't you? So you had no more reminders about what you did to me. Twice."

"I would understand if he killed you. After what you did. But, no." Beatriz shook her head. "I wouldn't prefer it. You are no more a reminder than every breath I take, aware that Daniel is not here to breathe as I do."

Renee glanced at Yakima. "She's always been a poetic little Spanish bitch."

Yakima glanced from Renee to Beatriz then indicated the former by canting his head at her. "Did you ride out here for this?"

"I don't know why I rode out here. I guess I felt that since I am who started it, I should be part of it."

"You're not who started it," Yakima said. "She is. She bought and paid for this whole thing herself. Her alone."

"Hey," Renee said. "I need a nature break. Kindly untie me you uncivilized savage."

Yakima walked over to her, slid his knife from its sheath, and sawed through the ropes binding her ankles. He glanced at the Yellowboy, which he'd leaned against a tree on the opposite side of the fire.

"Head out that way," he said, nodding toward the darkness beyond where Beatriz stood with her horse. "And don't go far because you won't get far."

Renee gave him a mock salute then walked away from him, giving Beatriz a sneer as she passed her, then faded into the brush and pines.

Yakima turned to Beatriz. "Cup of coffee? Best wait

and head back to town at dawn."

Beatriz tied her horse to a branch then walked up to the fire. Yakima squatted to pour her a cup of coffee and handed it to her. "Dangerous out here, with us," he told her. "You're taking a real chance."

"Like I said, I couldn't remain in town."

"Why?"

She only looked up at him, the firelight dancing in her soulful brown eyes.

Yeah, he knew why. She didn't need to say it. Damn complicated, her relationship with Renee.

Yakima sat on a log, facing the darkness into which Renee had gone to tend nature. He patted the place beside him. "Have a seat."

Beatriz sat down beside him. She sat sipping her coffee in silence.

Yakima kept his own counsel until, frowning suspiciously, he rose from the log and gazed out into the darkness where Renee had been for too long. "Hey, what are you doing out there?"

The only reply was the loud, metallic rasp of a rifle being cocked behind him.

Yakima wheeled. Renee stood by the tree against which he'd leaned the Yellowboy. She'd stolen around the camp in the darkness. The rifle was now in her hands. She stood crouched over it, legs spread, a devilish smile on her mouth, the fire flashing sharply in her hair and in her eyes.

"Renee!" Beatriz yelled.

She gained her feet and twisted around, stepping over the log. She dropped her coffee and thrust her hands out before her. "*Stop!*"

She stepped in front of Yakima at the same time the Winchester spoke.

She screamed as the bullet tore into her.

She fell backward into his arms.

Chapter 19

Renee stared down the Yellowboy's smoking barrel, her cold eyes quickly acquiring a shocked cast. She opened her hands. The Yellowboy dropped to the ground and Renee, unexpectedly, raised her hands to her temples, bent forward, and screamed, "*Nooo!*"

"Christ!" Yakima said as he eased Beatriz to the ground between the log and the fire.

"No!" Renee screamed again as she ran around the fire and knelt down beside the wounded woman.

Yakima ripped the bandanna from around his neck, wadded it up, and stuffed it into the bullet hole down low on Beatriz's left side and from which blood oozed up through the fabric of the cape she wore. She lay trembling, unconscious, head turned to one side.

"We have to get her to town," Yakima said. "She needs a sawbones fast!"

Renee just stared down in horror at the unconscious woman. Very gingerly, she raised her hand to her friend's face and slid a lock of hair away from Beatriz's left eye. Yakima studied her, puzzled. He could have sworn she'd regarded Beatriz as a blood enemy.

Had it all been a show? Or had she only thought Beatriz was her blood enemy but realized now, with Beatriz near death, that she'd been wrong, after all?

Yakima rose and gathered his gear then strode over to where Wolf stood hobbled in the trees south of the fire. He saddled and bridled the mount then grabbed his Winchester from where Renee had dropped it and shoved it into his saddle boot.

Renee remained on her knees beside Beatriz, still staring down at the woman in shock.

Yakima crouched, snaked one arm under Beatriz's neck, the other under her knees, and rose with her then set her up onto the saddle. He grabbed Wolf's reins then climbed up onto his back, behind Beatriz, and snaked one around her to hold her upright and to hold the bandanna against the wound. The ride might kill her, but he had little choice but to get her to a doctor fast, before she bled out. No doubt that bullet had ripped her up pretty bad inside; it needed to be taken out by someone wielding something more delicate than an Arkansas toothpick.

Renee rose and looked at him. "What about me?"

"It's over. Get the hell out of here."

"No." Renee shook her head. "I'm riding with you." As she hurried over to Renee's horse, she cast Yakima a cold glance. "And it's far from over."

"Have it your way." Yakima reined Wolf around and booted him into a trot through the trees and onto the trail to town.

He put Wolf into the fastest pace he dared in the night and with the injured woman sitting before him. He didn't look behind him, but he knew Renee was back there, matching his pace.

A few minutes after he'd started, Beatriz groaned and stirred, glancing up at him, the moonlight pooling in her eyes.

"Why in the hell did you take that bullet for me?" Yakima asked her. "It was my stupid mistake. I deserved that bullet!"

She reached up and placed her hand on his cheek. "I can't let another person die because of me."

"Dammit, when will you get it through your thick head that none of this is because of you? It's because of *her!*"

He cast a quick glance over his shoulder. Renee was loping her horse off of Wolf's left hip, staring at Yakima in that cold, indignant way of hers.

"It hurts," Beatriz said.

"I know. I'm sorry. Need to get you to town fast, though. You're losing blood."

Twenty minutes later, he slowed Wolf to a fast walk. As he did, he felt Beatriz's body slacken in his arms. He stopped Wolf, shook the woman gently. "Beatriz?"

Her head lolled back against his chest. She didn't open her eyes. He couldn't tell if she was breathing.

His heart thudded. "Beatriz?" he said again, louder.

Renee reined up beside him and cast her own worried gaze at the woman in Yakima's arms. "Beatriz!" Her voice was sharp, commanding, worried.

Beatriz's eyelids fluttered, opened. She looked at Renee.

"Just checkin' to make sure you're still with us," Yakima said, and booted Wolf ahead.

They galloped into town ten minutes later. The dawn was starting to paint the eastern horizon with a pale gray streak and windows of the houses and cabins of Lone Pine were starting to glow with lamplight. Yakima reined up at the doctor's office, in the second story of which Renee had informed him the doctor lived. It took little time to roust the man. Apparently, he was accustomed to business at odd hours. He ushered Yakima into one of the two examining rooms flanking his desk and then hazed both Yakima and Renee back outside.

They stood on the boardwalk in edgy silence until

Renee turned to him and said, "If she'd let me kill you, this would be over."

"You got some fight in you, don't you?"

She nodded as she stepped up to her horse. "Same as you." She swung up onto the sorrel's back. "I'm going home...but I'll be back with the remainder of my men. Whether she lives or dies"—she canted her head at the doctor's office—"we're gonna finish this thing right and proper."

"Savage rules we live by."

She reined her horse around and booted it in the direction of the livery barn where she'd acquire a fresh one for the ride to Bear Track. As she rode away, she tossed an arm up in acknowledgement.

"What happened?"

Yakima jerked with a start. He turned to see Pearl O'Malley step out of the shadows beside the doctor's office. She was dressed as usual—in men's rough trail gear. As usually, she wore it well. Her blond hair hung straight down from her men's felt hat to her shoulders.

"Do you ever go to bed?" Yakima asked her, incredulous.

"I'm lonely in bed without a man in it." Pearl stepped up to him and flicked her right index finger against the brim of his hat. "What happened?"

"Beatriz Salazar took a bullet meant for me."

"I heard you an' Renee were goin' at it like two bruins

warrin' over the same sow. Is it over?"

"No."

"Need some distraction?"

"Where's your old man?"

Pearl gave a devilish smile and drew her shoulders back so that her shirt drew taut across her breasts. "Usual place—in bed with a bottle."

Yakima took her hand in his and they set out for the livery barn.

***

Renee put her rented roan through the Bear Track portal and through the open gate. She looked around.

Two hands stood outside the bunkhouse, smoking and talking. One turned to see Renee then nudged the other one, who turned to her, as well, his eyes snapping wide in surprise.

"Boss!" he exclaimed taking one step forward.

As they both stood looking at her, two more stepped out of the bunkhouse behind them and then two more and then one more, donning their hats. They stood regarding their boss with mute surprise and incredulity.

"Renee!" a man called from the house.

She turned to see McGowan standing atop the porch steps, his right arm in a sling.

Renee booted her horse over to where the seven hands stood out front of the bunkhouse, watching her, and reined up before them. "Are you all that's left?" she asked with sharp scolding in her voice.

"'Fraid so," said the one named Watt Jennings, a tall, rather attractive, blue-eyed man in his late-twenties and said to have been a former firebrand gunslinger from New Mexico with a bounty on his head.

Renee shook her head with open contempt then booted her horse over to the house and looked up at McGowan gazing down from the porch at her. He wasn't wearing his hat and his hair wasn't combed. His shirttails were out of his pants, and the shirt was unbuttoned, showing his wash-worn longhandle top beneath it.

"Renee," he said again, frowning, puzzled. "How'd you...?"

She glanced past him to see a bottle sitting beside a chair to the left of the front door. He turned to follow her glance then returned his gaze to her. "For the pain."

"Twenty men," she said with cold accusing. "Twenty men and I have eight left? And they're not out looking for me?"

The foreman flushed, shook his head. "He's damn crafty. We were going to take a break. As you can see, I'm a bit out of commission."

"You're useless but not out of commission. Only dead

men can't ride. Haul your gear back to the bunkhouse, Garth. Get the men ready to ride first thing in the morning." Renee swung down from the horse's back and dropped the reins. "Put up my horse." She climbed the porch steps. As she brushed past him she curled her upper lip and added, "Send Jennings to the house. He'll be taking your place."

Renee walked into the house and, shaking out her hair, climbed the stairs to the second story. When he arrived, she would have Jennings heat water for her bath. She'd let him scrub her back for her, too, she thought with a devious little quirk of her mouth corners. She started to walk past Weldon's room on her right then glanced at the door and stopped.

She placed her hand on the door, splayed her fingers across the wood.

She lowered her hand to the knob, twisted it, and pushed it open. She stood staring inside at her son's bed, dresser, chest of drawers, the ladderback chair by the window. It remained as he'd last left it, clothes and tack and guns and ammunition strewn about, the bed unmade. Disheveled as it was, she'd wanted to leave it exactly as he'd left it.

Her eyes found a carved wooden horse on the floor amidst the clutter. She walked over to it and picked it up. She held it in her hands, staring down at it. Weldon had carved the horse when he'd been a very young boy, not even ten years old. He'd been a gifted child. Most didn't know that side of him. They saw only what came later. But what came later had come because of what had happened to his father.

It hadn't been Weldon's fault how he'd turned out.

It was Beatriz's fault.

So why, then, had Renee been so horrified at having shot her?

Because she was all Renee had. And at one time, way back in their girlhood years, they'd been so much more than friends—until Renee's father had found them together and had whipped them both.

That had put an end to that aspect of their relationship, and Renee had married the next closest person to her—Daniel. She'd found herself falling in love with him. Real, genuine love. It had made up for losing Beatriz.

And then the two closest people to her betrayed her together.

Still, Beatriz was all she had. She'd realized for the first time last night that she hated and loved her.

A knock on the front door jerked her out of her reverie.

She kissed the horse and set it on the dresser.

She left Weldon's room, closing the door behind her, and went downstairs.

Late that night, the cat-like screams woke McGowan

up in the bunkhouse, and he winced at the mauling Jennings was getting. He took a slug of whiskey, rolled over, wincing at the pain in his shoulder, and fell back into painful asleep.

up in the bunkhouse, and he winced at the nagging
over, wincing at the pain in his shoulder, and fell back
into painful sleep.

Chapter 20

In the straw mound in the livery barn, Yakima opened
his eyes.

He turned to see Pearl lying belly down beside him, her
hair a pretty, flaxen tumbleweed about her head. A single
horse blanket only partly covered them both. It exposed
her bare shoulders and part of her slender back. In the
pale light of dawn pushing through a near window, her
skin was as pink as a ripe peach.

Yakima rose onto a shoulder, leaned over, swept her
hair aside with one hand, and planted a tender kiss on
the back of her neck.

Cheek pressed against the straw, she smiled but did
not open her eyes.

"Good morning," she said in a sleep-husky voice.

"Mornin', darlin'. You stayed."

Smiling, she nodded, making a rustling sound in

the straw.

"Your pa's gonna shoot me, an' I reckon I deserve it."

"He won't be up till noon. Besides..." She turned to face him and sandwiched his big, chiseled face between her hands. "Wasn't it worth it?"

Yakima smiled nodded. "Every bit. Renee Stratton's gonna be mighty mad, though. She wants that privilege to herself."

He tossed the blanket aside and heaved himself to his feet. He stood tall and naked, stretching his arms high above his head, yawning. He gave Wolf's rump an affectionate slap and said, "Mornin', you ol' broomtail!"

Wolf turned his head to give him an incredulous look.

Pearl rose to her knees and kissed and fondled Yakima.

"Stop that, now," he said, chuckling, reaching for his underwear. "I gotta get a move on."

"Where you goin'?" she said, crawling around on her hands and knees, following him, hugging his bare left leg and pressing a tender kiss to the side of the bandaged brand.

"Toward Bear Track."

"*Bear Track?* Why? You really are just plain suicidal, Yakima!"

"Nope. Suicide would be getting run down in town, boxed into a corner. I'm gonna ride out and find some high ground. If it's gonna be eight against one, I need

215

an advantage."

"Can I come with you? I can shoot. Ask Pa!"

Yakima smiled down at her gently, shook his head. "I fight my own fights."

"Men!" Pearl pouted, pounding the ends of her fists against her bare thighs.

Yakima chuckled and continued dressing.

She scuttled back on her little pink butt and leaned back against the stall partition. She drew her knees to her breasts and folded her arms around them. "I don't want you to die alone out there, Yakima. You're a good sort, but I got a feelin' you're alone most of the time." Looking up at him with genuine concern, she shook her head. A sheen of tears shone in her eyes. "A man shouldn't die alone. 'Specially a good man. 'Specially one who doesn't deserve to be treated this way."

"Thank you, honey." Yakima shook out his shirt and drew it around his shoulders. "I 'spect I was destined to die alone."

No, he'd been destined to die with Faith, but he'd been robbed of her, she of him.

Pearl watched him dress and saddle Wolf in sullen silence.

He opened the stable door to back Wolf out into the alley and turned to Pearl. She remained sitting there, nude, against the stall partition. He walked over, crouched to kiss her cheek. "Goodbye, honey."

She looked at him, mouth corners drawn down, nodding sadly.

Yakima backed Wolf out of the stall then opened the big stock doors and led him outside. He set some coins on the lid of the water barrel in payment for Flynn's services then mounted up, reined Wolf around, and booted him into a trot down the street filled with dawn shadows and very little movement.

He rode into the countryside and booted the horse into a rocking lope. When he was a mile from town, he began closely surveying the country on both sides of the trail. Several stone escarpments, low mesas, and haystack buttes rose around him. He continued riding, looking for the right formation from which to wage the war.

As he put Lone Pine farther behind him, the sun poked up above the horizon, bathing the bristling desert around him with salmon light and cool, blue shadows.

He rounded a curve and climbed a steep hill. As he crested the hill, he jerked Wolf to an abrupt halt and stared down the hill's other side, heart thudding.

There they were—all nine of them, including Renee, who rode in the lead with a tall, lean, rakishly handsome young man in a low-crowned black hat and with two pistols bristling on his hips. McGowan rode back with the others, looking old and miserable, his arm in a sling.

Renee and her new foreman were just starting up the hill. As they did, their hat brims came up to reveal their faces bathed in the orange-salmon light of the rising sun. Their eyes widened when they saw Yakima, and they jerked their mounts to such sudden stops that McGowan's horse rammed into Renee's from behind.

"Whoa!" the wounded man said, frowning at his boss then following her gaze to the ridge crest. He cursed and slid his carbine from his saddle boot.

Yakima curveted Wolf and gazed down at his adversaries. He grinned.

"Out bright an' early, I see."

Renee just stared at him with those stony eyes.

She hardened her jaws, gritted her teeth, and said, "Get that son of a bitch!"

Yakima slid his own Winchester from its saddle sheath, cocked it, snapped it to his shoulder, took hasty aimed, and fired.

Too hasty.

The man he'd been aiming at—the one Yakima assumed was Renee's new foreman—leaned to one side as he reached for his own rifle and the bullet merely sliced across the side of his neck to pass between two of the other riders and plume dust on the trail behind him.

The man cursed, slapped his gloved hand to his neck, and glared up at Yakima, raising his own Winchester, as were all of the others now, as well.

Yakima jerked Wolf around and booted him into a hard run as rifles thundered behind him and bullets stitched the air around his head before he'd put the hill between him and the Bear Track riders. Descending the hill and then flattening out on the trail below, he looked for cover. He probably shouldn't have been so choosy before. Now he had a wolf pack nipping at his heels.

Casting his gaze off the trail's right side, he spied what appeared an arroyo fringed with rocks and scrub a hundred yards off the trail. He turned Wolf toward it as rifles belched behind him and hooves thundered. Bullets kicked up dust around him as he galloped Wolf, weaving him, trying to make it a challenge for his pursuers to draw beads on him.

Still, one bullet burned across the outside of his right arm.

"Come on, boy," Yakima said, whipping his rein ends against Wolf's right hip. "Give it all ya got!"

Wolf put his head down and laid his ears back as he lunged ahead even faster, pulling the ground back behind him with his scissoring hooves. As the rifle reports grew less loud, Yakima cast a glance over his right shoulder. Wolf was widening the gap between him and Yakima and the Bear Track riders. Through the haze of Wolf's billowing dust, Yakima saw them galloping, hunkered low and spread out in shaggy line, no longer taking time to fire now but concentrating on trying to overtake him.

Yakima turned his head forward, glad none of his stalkers had a horse with as much speed and bottom as Wolf did.

He found a gap in the brush and aimed Wolf for it. Then he was through it and Wolf went airborne, descending the five-foot-high bank to land in the sandy, gravelly bottom of the dry wash below.

Yakima reined the horse to a skidding halt then threw his right leg over the horn, dropped to the ground, and spanked Wolf off down the arroyo and out of the line of fire. Yakima scrambled up the cutbank, removed his hat, and edged a look over the top. The Bear Track riders were seventy yards away and closing fast—a jostling line of silhouetted horses and riders coming hell for leather, one man just then losing his hat to the wind.

Yakima jacked a round into the Winchester, laid the barrel out on the ground before him, lined up the sights on the riders blurred by the glare of the intensifying morning son, and fired. One of the riders in the middle of the pack threw his arms up with a yelp and, tossing away his rifle, rolled over his horse's arched tail to pinwheel wildly before striking the ground.

One of the others yelled, "Whoah! Whoah! Whoah! He's in the wash!"

As they drew their own mounts down to skidding

halts and leaped from their saddles, Yakima tried to pick out a target. It wasn't easy, as they were all moving fast, looking around and scrambling for cover—rocks, cedars, low hummocks of ground lying about fifty yards from Yakima's position. They were further obscured by their horses' billowing dust.

Yakima fired at one of the scrambling riders as the man ran for a large, white rock, but his bullet appeared to only clip the man's boot heel just before the man dove forward and crawled quickly out of sight behind the rock.

Yakima ejected the spent cartridge, which flashed in the sunshine as it winged back behind him and pumped a fresh one into the Winchester's action. He pulled his head down behind the cutbank as the Bear Track men and woman returned fire, the bullets kicking up dust and sod at the lip of the bank and ripping branches off the surrounding brush.

Suddenly, the thunder stopped.

In the silence that descended in its wake, Renee yelled, "You're just prolonging the inevitable, you know!"

Yakima turned his head sideways to the cutbank, keeping it beneath the crest so he didn't get it shot off, and yelled, "Aren't we all?"

"Very funny!"

"Why don't you throw your rifles down and come out in the open where I can line up my sights on you?

Make it quicker that way!"

A rifle spoke. The slug clipped the lip of the cutbank, pelting Yakima's head with dirt and grass.

"Is that a no?" he yelled.

He crabbed through the brush to his left, wanting to change his position. When he was roughly five feet from where he'd been before, he quickly snaked the rifle up over the lip, lined up his sights on a hatted head poking up above a low hummock of sage-covered ground, and fired.

The man's head jerked back out of sight as he tossed his rifle in the air.

One of the others cursed.

Yakima yelled, "Now you're down to seven!" and drew his head below the cutbank again as they tore into his new position with their rifles.

Staying low, Yakima scrambled back to his original position and edged a cautious look over the cutbank's lip. He fired at one of the shooters but his bullet only smashed into the face of the rock behind which the man was firing. With that quick look, however, he'd glimpsed the unmistakable flame-red hair of his principal tormentor cowing behind a low shelf of weed-tufted ground just as she, having seen Yakima's smoke puff, slid her rifle toward him.

Yakima jerked his head down again as her bullet brushed the lip and thudded into the floor of the arroyo behind him. The closeness of that bullet impressed upon him her prowess with a long gun and made him consider reneging on his promise to let her live.

He might have to rethink that.

On the other hand, she'll likely give him no other choice.

He chuckled dryly to himself as he pressed his back against the embankment. "Nothin' like countin' your chickens before they're hatched!"

The corner of his right eye picked up movement down the arroyo in that direction. Was one of them using the others' covering fire to try to sneak around him?

As bullets continued to smash through the brush around him and plume sand on the arroyo's floor, Yakima slid slowly down the bank on his butt.

He stopped at the edge of the brush and snaked a look around and down the arroyo on his right. He could see only forty feet or so; beyond that the arroyo curved sharply to the right.

A shadow moved on the ground just before that bend in the ravine's brush-stippled wall. A half an eye wink later a man appeared, crouching low and aiming a carbine out in front of him. He wore a cream hat and a red-checked shirt and green neckerchief and brown chaps.

Yakima got only the briefest of glimpses of him, because he jerked his head back behind the brush wall quickly. He held the Yellowboy close before him, pressing the top of the barrel against his forehead, waiting...

Chapter 21

Yakima counted to ten then thrust his rifle out around the brush, aiming down the arroyo.

A rifle thundered before his did—the rifle of the man only ten feet away from him now and sticking close to the brush on the sloping embankment. The bullet tore into Yakima's left arm—a powerful, burning blow that made him drop the Yellowboy.

The man before him whooped victoriously and cocked his rifle again.

Yakima threw himself out onto the arroyo floor and rolled once, barely avoiding another coring. As he rolled up on his right side, he fought against the pain in his left arm to use his right hand to palm his Colt, cock, aim, and fire.

His stalker jerked back as the bullet punched into his chest. His eyes rolled back in his head as he staggered backward, tripped over his spurs, and fell.

Yakima cursed as he held his gun hand to his left arm, up high near the shoulder, feeling the warm blood oozing. As he did, he picked up movement in the arroyo again, this time in the opposite direction from the approach of the bastard who'd shot him.

Again, he raised the Colt and cocked it but held fire, frowning down the barrel. The slender rider galloping toward him from around a bend in the arroyo to the east had long, flaxen hair which blew back in the wind as Pearl approached on a sleek steeldust mare.

"Pearl, get back!" Yakima yelled, trying to keep his voice low, waving the hand that still held the gun.

Pearl checked the steeldust down. "Yakima!"

She leaped out of the saddle and, sliding a Winchester carbine from a saddle sheath, came running.

"No, get back!" Yakima yelled again, hoping Renee's men didn't hear though they'd probably already heard Pearl.

Pearl came running and dropped to a knee beside Yakima. "You're hit!"

"What the hell are you doing out here? You're gonna get yourself killed!"

"So are you!" she said, ripping her red bandanna from around her neck and tying it over the wound in Yakima's arm.

"Please, Pearl—get back to town. There's not much

time!"

Pearl rose and tugged on Yakima right arm, rocking back on the heels of her boots. "Come on! I got an idea!"

"Huh?"

"Come on, Yakima! Like you said, there's not much time!" she said, casting her gaze through the brush toward where the shooting had been coming from. "I saw Wolf down yonder. Let's get you to him!"

"I'm gonna stay and finish this!"

She gave another powerful tug on his arm. "If you stay, they'll finish *you*!"

"Ah, hell." She likely had a point. He didn't like the silence he heard from the Bear Track riders. They were likely closing on the arroyo, fingers curled through their Winchesters' trigger guards.

Yakima let Pearl help him to his feet and then, gritting his teeth against the pain in his burning arm, he followed her, running at a crouch, over to where the steeldust stood regarding them skeptically, reins trailing to the ground. She grabbed the reins, climbed into the saddle, and extended her hand to Yakima, who took it and clambered onto the horse, behind her.

She reined the buckskin around, clucked it into a trot and then a gallop, following the arroyo around two bends before Wolf appeared, idly cropping grass along the arroyo's north bank. Yakima stepped gingerly down from the steeldust then, clutching his gloved hand over the bandanna Pearl had knotted around his arm, he stumbled over to Wolf, grabbed the reins, and swung up into the saddle.

He reined Wolf around to face Pearl. "Where we goin'?"

"Follow me."

Pearl booted the steeldust on down the arroyo.

Gritting his teeth against the pain in his arm while applying pressure with his right hand, trying to get the bleeding to slow, Yakima followed her. He cast cautious glances behind him, knowing that Renee's men would be on their trail soon. They rode for several minutes, galloping, before Pearl swung the steeldust to the right and followed a game path up out of the arroyo.

Yakima followed her out of the arroyo and put Wolf into a gallop behind her, heading for a canyon opening in a ridge wall a hundred yards beyond. He followed her into the canyon, which was narrow, circuitous, and stone floored, with a boulder-strewn dry wash running along the ridge wall on their left. A quarter mile into the canyon, Pearl crossed the dry wash and put the buckskin up a ridge that quickly grew forested. The horses climbed hard for several hundred yards before they crossed a talus slide then swung onto a two-track wagon trail.

The air was cooler here than below, and rife with pine tang. Squirrels yammered from branches at the intruders.

They followed the trail around the belly of the mountain until another canyon yawned ahead on Yakima's right.

"Follow me," Pearl said, and put the buckskin down the canyon's sloping, rocky wall.

Yakima followed her into the pine- and boulder-choked canyon. This canyon was narrower than the first, its stony walls coming to life with ancient pictographs. A spring trickled down through boulders to pool in a stone tank at the base of the ridge and then to run down a narrow trough that had likely been cut by the spring over the centuries. The water smelled like mushrooms and minerals.

He followed Pearl under a stone arch also decorated with pictographs and then down through more cool pines into yet another canyon, as narrow as the last one and also cut by a slow, dark stream. Ahead, a stone cabin with a woven pine brush roof appeared. Behind the cabin lay the dark oval of a mine shaft. The area around the cabin and the mine was strewn with slag and littered with old mining implements including a rusting, overturned rail car.

As Pearl reined up in front of the cabin, Yakima jerked Wolf to a sudden stop. He'd heard something. He pricked his ears, listening. A low rumble rose and then dwindled back to silence.

Pearl glanced at Yakima. "That was them. They rode on past the canyon. They probably think we're headed for an old line shack on Spider Mountain. They likely don't know about this place. I don't think anyone does but me. Me an' the fella that built it, that is. I stumbled on it while following an elk I'd shot several years back."

Yakima gave a wry snort as he dismounted. This girl was pretty, for sure, but she had the bark on.

"They'll find us here soon. Renee won't give up. She's losing and she doesn't like losing—especially to the man who killed her son."

"We'll get you tended and ready for her." Pearl strode to the cabin. "Come on. The cabin's right cozy. I come out here now and then when I get sick to death of Pa and town."

She gingerly opened the cabin door, which was attached to the frame by only the upper hinge and stepped inside. "Home sweet home," she said.

Yakima unsheathed his Yellowboy and followed her inside. The cabin was cozy. Not only cozy with a cot, a rocking chair, an eating table, and a sheet-iron stove, but comfortable. There were a pillow and blankets on the cot and the shelves in the kitchen area were stocked with canned goods and burlap sacks of drygoods. Shirts and old denim trousers hung from pegs and two sets of high-topped, lace-up miners' boots were parked neatly on a mat by the door. A pair of deerskin moccasins sat on the hemp rug beside the rocking chair.

"Are you sure this place is abandoned?"

"It's abandoned, all right," Pearl said, shoving sticks and branches into the stove from a pile against the wall behind it. "But the fella who lived here didn't go far."

Yakima slacked into a chair with a grunt and frowned at her, curious.

Pearl looked at him and canted her head toward the cabin's rear wall. "He's in the mine. Nothin' but strewn bones around a pick and a shovel. He musta been workin' in there an' died of a heart stroke or some such. Coyotes or wildcats must have had 'em a good supper that night."

"Damn the luck."

"There's a poke of gold dust in one of the cabinets," Pearl said. "That's how I know no one's been here but me since the old fella died. I left it there because it's bad luck to steal from dead folks."

"Did the old fella stock any whiskey? I sure could use a pull," Yakima said.

"He did."

Pearl grabbed a flat, brown bottle off a shelf near the stove and set it on the table. Yakima pried the cork from the bottle.

"Rags?"

"Got them, too."

She produced the rags from a low shelf near the floor, shook the dust out of them, and set them on the table, as well.

"Thanks mighty kindly." Yakima took a pull from the bottle. It burned going down but soothed when it reached his belly.

"Now you're happy I showed up," Pearl said, giving him an impudent smile. Having built a fire in the ticking and sighing stove, she closed the door.

"No, I'm not, darlin'." Yakima untied the bandanna from over his wound and unsheathed his Bowie knife. "I don't want you takin' a bullet meant for me, so when Renee shows, you keep your head down—understand?"

"I told you I know how to handle that rifle."

As he raised the Bowie to his arm, he gave her a hard, commanding look. "You do as I say or I'll paddle your bottom."

"Sounds like fun!" Pearl laughed. She sat in a chair beside him and ran a hand through his long, sweat-damp hair. "How you feelin', Yakima?"

"A little worse for the wear is all."

"You want me to do that for you?"

Turning the Bowie upside down, he poked the curved tip through the blood-soaked cloth of his shirt and began cutting the material around the wound. "Nah. I've kept in good practice over the years, sad to say. At least the bullet went all the way through. I'm just gonna clean it, cauterize it, an' call it good."

He set the knife down and peeled the bloody swatch of

cut fabric away from the hole in his arm. Blood was still oozing up out of it, but it had slowed some. It dribbled down the side of his arm to stain the two cloths he'd set on the table beneath it. He picked up the bottle and, wincing at the anticipated burn, turned it over and let the amber liquid flow over the bloody hole.

He and Pearl, watching closely, both sucked air sharply through their teeth.

He turned his arm over and poured the whiskey over the exit wound, as well.

Again, he and Pearl sucked air through their teeth.

The burn wasn't as bad as the branding, but it reminded him of it. It also reminded him that he'd not only been branded by Renee Stratton, but now he'd been shot by her, too. Maybe by one of her men, but she owned that bullet every bit as much as she owned that branding iron. She'd started the war. He was just fighting back.

He wrapped a clean rag around the wound, took another pull from the bottle, and wrapped his left hand around his arm, over the cloth, applying pressure.

"Honey," he said, his voice husky with pain, "would you please set my knife in the stove?"

"Oh, boy," Pearl said darkly and scooped the knife off the table.

She squatted to open the stove door and set the blade inside, over the crackling and popping flames.

"Get it good and hot," Yakima said. "When the blade glows, it's ready."

Waiting for the blade to heat, Yakima kept a cautious eye on the open front door, watching for Renee. He hoped she held off. He needed to cauterize the wound or he was doomed.

"Here you go," Pearl said softly, setting the glowing blade on the table by Yakima.

He lifted the blade by the handle. Suddenly, it wasn't his Bowie knife anymore.

It was the glowing Bear Track brand.

He removed the cloth, laid the blade against his flesh, setting his leg on fire all over again.

He and Pearl groaned.

His flesh was still smoking around both wounds—he imagined it was smoking around the brand, as well—when the thunder of oncoming riders rose.

Chapter 22

Yakima had just heard the hoof thuds before, passing out, his head hit the table with a *bang!*

"Yakima!" he heard Pearl yell as though from far away.

Yakima fought off the chains of unconscious, lifted his head and, suppressing the raging burn in his arm, grabbed his Winchester off the table.

He looked around the cabin, and his heart thudded. He spoke as though around marbles in his mouth. "We have to hole up outside. Can't get trapped in here. With that pine roof, they'll burn us out."

"The mine!" Pearl grabbed his good arm. "Come on!"

Leaning on the girl, who'd grabbed her own rifle, Yakima staggered outside and peered up canyon the way he and Pearl had come. He could hear the riders, the hoofbeats growing louder but couldn't see them yet. Staggering, almost falling, he went over and slapped

Wolf's rump, sending the horse on down the canyon. He slapped the rump of Pearl's mount, then, too, and the steeldust put its head down, kicked out a back foot, and lunged on down canyon after Wolf.

Both horses disappeared around a bend.

"Let's go!" Yakima said, wrapping his arm around Pearl's shoulders and leaning into her again.

"Here we go!" Pearl said and began leading him around behind the cabin.

They climbed a slope beneath the mine portal, slipping on the slag. The thunder of the oncoming riders grew louder, and Yakima could hear the squawk of tack now, too.

Just before stepping inside the mine, he cast a quick look over his right shoulder. Just then the riders galloped out from around a pile of boulders and thundered toward the cabin.

"There!" yelled one of the men riding behind the redheaded Renee and her new foreman, thrusting his arm and jutting finger toward Yakima and Pearl.

"Damn!" Yakima said, and continued on into the mine, leaning on Pearl, the darkness sweeping over and around him with the smell of rotting wood, dead rodents, and damp stone. "They saw us!"

Yakima stopped, removed his arm from around Pearl, and took his Winchester in both hands, turning to face the entrance. "Gonna have to hold 'em off…" He let the words die on his lips as the mine swirled around him and he staggered to one side, ramming a shoulder against the chiseled stone wall.

"You're in no condition!" Pearl said, leaning into him again, wrapping his right arm around her shoulders, leading him farther into the mine.

Behind him, hooves drummed again and then he heard Renee yell something. Running footsteps sounded then, growing quickly louder.

"Gotta…go…faster," Yakima grunted out, increasing his pace though he felt as though over the past hour he'd chugged two jugs of cheap whiskey.

Pearl quickened her own pace beside him.

"They'll shoot in here, fill us with so much lead…" Yakima drawled. "Any cover?"

"A little farther along there's the start of an intersecting mine." Pearl's voice, shrill with fear, echoed around them.

Behind them, boots clacked on rock. There was the rasping of strained breathing as Renee and her men scrambled up the slope toward the mine.

"Hold on." Yakima removed his arm from around Pearl's shoulders and swung around, staggering only a little now. The direness of the situation was an effective bracer. He pumped a round into the Winchester's chamber.

A man's hatted head and shoulders appeared, rising up from the slope below the mine.

The Yellowboy bucked and thundered in Yakima's hands.

The man who'd just then straightened after pushing up off the decline, and was holding a Winchester, was blown back down the slope and into another man, who wailed and lost his hat and fell beneath the man Yakima had shot.

"Yakima!" Pearl grabbed his arm and pulled him into the niche where the old prospector must have started chipping out an intersecting shaft.

Just as they stepped into the niche, rifles began belching loudly back toward the entrance. Bullets screeched through the near-dark shaft that Yakima and Pearl had just left.

"Close one," Pearl said, breathing hard beside Yakima.

"Yeah. But they're down to four now." Yakima dropped to a knee at the edge of the niche as rifles continued thundering at the entrance and bullets shrilled ominously past him to smash into the stony end of the main mine to his left. "Manageable."

He dropped to his belly and edged a look around the edge of the niche. All four remaining riders stood silhouetted against the mine entrance, firing their Winchesters, red flames lapping from the barrels.

Yakima slid his rifle up and around the corner, cocked it, and aimed toward the four shooters. Renee stood second from left, distinguishable by her diminutive size and her red hair. Yakima had to use his left hand though it burned all the way from the wound into the hand. Using his right hand would require him to shove too much of himself into the main mine and risk getting beheaded by a bullet.

He wished his old Shaolin friend, Ralph, had taught him pain suppression.

He lined up his sights on the man standing beside Renee, probably her new foreman. He drew back his left index finger against the trigger.

The Yellowboy leaped and roared, enflaming the misery in that arm.

The man moved at the same time Yakima tripped the trigger, and the bullet smashed off the receiver of the rifle in his hands. He screamed and dropped the rifle, jerking his head back as though the ricochet had caught him in the face. He twisted around and dropped to his knees, cupping a hand over his left eye.

Yakima cursed and clumsily, his left arm and hand shaking, rammed another round into the chamber but by the time he got the rifle set against his shoulder again, the three other shooters had abandoned the mine entrance. One man quickly grabbed the man Yakima had shot and dragged him away from the entrance before Yakima could draw a steady bead on him.

Silence filled the mine.

"What happened?" Pearl whispered behind Yakima.

"Shh."

He pricked his ears, listening.

From the entrance, he could hear them talking but too quietly for him to be able to make out what they were saying. One man was groaning and cursing—the man Yakima had shot.

A gun popped. The groaning died.

Yakima hooked a crooked smile. He'd have bet gold dust to cheap beer that Renee had put the man out of his misery, likely just to stop his infernal caterwauling.

Only three now...

The talking stopped.

Again, silence.

Yakima spied movement at the far left side of the entrance.

Thud!

"What the hell is she doing?"

He saw the flicker of movement again. A sledge-hammer?

Thud!

Now he clearly saw the head of the sledgehammer as someone smashed it against the moldering leg of the wood framing supporting the mine's stone roof.

Yakima's heart hiccupped.

She was trying to cave in the mine!

"What is that?" Pearl asked behind him.

Yakima snapped his rifle up, but he had no target. All he could see was the head of the hammer someone—likely Renee herself, judging by the feminine tone of the grunts that accompanied each whack—was smashing against the ceiling support post.

"Damn!"

The epithet had no sooner left his lips than a loud, chilling cracking noise rose. The ceiling support post partly jackknifed, debris tumbling from the ceiling into the entrance.

Again, he saw the arc of the sledgehammer as someone smashed it once more against the post. This time the post gave way and more debris rained down. More ceiling beams dropped, as well, and then suddenly a great roar filled Yakima's ears as the oval-shaped, sunshine-filled mine entrance suddenly turned dark.

The floor trembled beneath Yakima's belly.

His guts turned to ice as he stared, unblinking, at the churning darkness before him. A great cloud of dust that smelled like dirt and ancient wood roiled over him, filling his nose and eyes.

"Oh, my God!" Pearl cried. "What happened?"

The rain of rock and wood gradually dwindled to silence. A couple of more bits of debris clattered and thudded on to the mine floor. Then, again, silence.

This time total. It matched the total darkness.

***

Minutes earlier, Renee had cocked and fired her Winchester into the dark mine.

Her mouth corners quirked in delight as she imagined the half-breed shredded by the lead she and her remaining men—McGowan, Jennings, and Ty Learner—were throwing at him.

She couldn't see him, of course. Too dark beyond the first twenty feet or so. Still, she could see him in her mind's eye, dancing as the bullets ripped into him before he fell and rolled and yet more lead hammered into him, finished him once and for all.

The man who'd taken her son from her! The man who by his infernal Indian cunning had killed nearly all of her men!

To her left rose a raking *ping!* And then Watt Jennings screamed, dropped his rifle, and twisted around, giving his back to the mine, and fell to his knees.

"Woah!" Ty Learner cried to Renee's right and darted away from the mine entrance.

Garth McGowan stepped away from the mine entrance on Renee's left.

Renee side-stepped to her right and glanced at Learner, pointing at Jennings, who sat cupping his hand to his left eye. "Grab him!"

Learner reached past Renee, quickly grabbed Jenning's left arm and pulled him clear of the mine entrance. Jennings dropped to his knees again, moaning and shouting, "My eye!"

Ignoring him, Renee shot her exasperated gaze to McGowan standing on the other side of the mine entrance. His left arm was in a sling and blood stained his shirt over that shoulder. He stared back at Renee, mute jeering in his gaze as though to say, "See? Shoulda put a bullet in him."

Speaking of putting a bullet in someone...

Renee turned to where Jennings knelt, wailing and clutching his eye. She grabbed her Winchester, racked a round into the chamber, aimed quickly, and drilled a round through the back of Jennings' head.

"Woah!" Learner said, leaping back in astonishment.

"Renee!" McGowan said.

Ignoring him, she set the rifle down.

She turned to the mine again, gave a frustrated groan and looked around at the debris around her—slag and rocks and old mining implements. Spying a rusty sledgehammer, she walked over and picked it up.

She gave another frustrated groan as she hefted the hammer in her hands. She stepped up to the portal's right corner. The ceiling support post before her was badly rotted, gray, and splintery.

She glanced at McGowan again who continued to study her without expression but with a lingering darkness in his eyes. The poor, pathetic bastard, drunk from all the whiskey he drank to keep the pain in his wounded shoulder at bay, was a mere husk of his former self. She knew it and he knew it, and he was blaming her for it. He wouldn't say that, of course, but it was in his eyes.

Renee hated that look. What had she been supposed to do? *Not* exact revenge for her only child's murder?

Renee spread her boots and swung the hammer back behind her left shoulder.

She gave a loud, angry grunt as she swung it forward, smashing the rusty head against the post. There was a thud and a cracking sound. The post and several ceiling beams, spaced five feet apart, shuddered and creaked.

Renee raised the sledgehammer again and with another grunt she swung it forward.

Thud-Crack!

Again: Thud-Crackkk!

The post gave slightly in the middle, the post above the crack leaning forward, the post below the crack leaning backward.

Dust sifted down from the mine ceiling between the quivering beams.

Again, Renee raised the sledgehammer, swung it forward harder than before, with an even louder grunt.

The post gave. Renee stepped back as the ceiling beams and the rock it had been supporting collapsed onto the mine floor with a great peal of roaring thunder. Dust mushroomed out of the portal, as thick as morning fog on a lake.

"There!" she said to McGowan and threw down the hammer. "Dead and buried!"

Chapter 23

Yakima dug a sulfur-tipped match out of his shirt pocket and scratched it to life on his thumbnail.

Spitting grit from his lips, he shoved the match forward, spreading the watery sphere of flickering light straight out before him until it slid over the pile of rock and splintered wood beams.

Standing to his right, Pearl gasped and closed her hands over her mouth.

"Damn," Yakima said.

"Oh, my God!"

Pearl dashed forward and began grabbing rocks and chunks of wood and throwing them back behind her. She worked with furious desperation, sobbing and grunting, breathing hard.

"Pearl," Yakima said. "Stop."

Pearl continued throwing rocks behind her until she

grabbed the edge of a huge rock slab that would not budge. She pulled on it hard with both hands, sobbing.

"Come on, damn you—*move*!" she cried.

Yakima's match burned down to his fingers. He dropped it and fired another one. Still Pearl was trying to pull back on the slab, sobbing.

Yakima placed his hand on her shoulder. "Pearl…it's no use. Half the mine is caved in. We're not gonna get out that way."

Pearl gave a horrified yowl, rose, turned to him and threw her arms around his neck, sobbing against his chest. "What are we gonna do, Yakima?"

Yakima dropped the match and wrapped his good arm around her. "All we can, honey. All we can."

He patted her back.

"I'm so frightened!" She shuddered against him.

"Yeah, I gotta admit it's a frightening situation."

"I don't wanna die! Not like this!"

"We're not going to, honey." Yakima placed his right hand on her shoulder and shoved her gently out away from him, staring down at her in the darkness though he could just barely see her outline in the stygian blackness. "Do you know how much farther the main shaft goes into the mountain?"

"No," she said, sniffing. "I've never been all the way in. When I found the old prospector's bones, that was far enough for me."

Yakima gave a wry snort. "All right." He trailed his hand down her arm to her hand and squeezed it. "Come on. Let's check it out."

Letting his left arm hang at his side, he dug another lucifer out of his shirt pocket and snapped it to life. It flared, spreading the flickering glow on the floor and chiseled stone walls. He and Pearl started walking, avoiding dead bats and rodents and rock that had tumbled from the ceiling.

He'd had to snap another match to life when more debris appeared on the floor before him. He stopped, looked down, grimacing.

This debris was strewn bones to which bits of denim and wool clung. Nearby lay a pick, a billed immigrant cap, and one badly battered hobnail boot from the top of which a white leg bone protruded.

"That's him," Pearl said with a shudder.

"Poor ol' devil. Come on," Yakima said. "Let's keep goin'."

They continued walking, following a slight curve in the shaft. After a half-dozen steps, Yakima stopped and stared ahead, his heartbeat increasing hopefully. A slender strip of sunlight lay at a slant on the floor about twenty feet ahead of him.

"Sunlight!" Pearl thrilled.

Yakima dropped the match and hurried forward to stare down at the ray of light, which was about six feet long and four inches wide. He lifted his gaze to the ceiling. That's where the light was penetrating the mine, through a fissure running from the middle of the ceiling to where the ceiling met the wall, at a forward slant.

Just beyond the light was solid rock. It was the end of the shaft.

Yakima pondered the crack. The light was a little weak, which meant it must be angling down through a deep crack or a natural flue in the mountain. Beyond the crack lay a larger opening, funnel-shaped and stretching up to the top of the mountain and the sky at an easy slant. Staring up through the crack, it appeared the cleft or flue was only a few feet above the crack in the ceiling.

So close and yet so far.

"What do you think, Yakima?" Pearl said in a frightened little girl's voice.

"I think we'd have to lose a lot of weight to get out that way."

Pearl released a ragged sigh.

Yakima walked over to where the ceiling met the wall. There was a downward slanting slab in the ceiling near the crack. Yakima pondered it.

He reached up with his right hand, stuck his fingers into the crack and was able to get a grip on the slab. He pulled, gritting his teeth. He pulled harder, grinding his teeth together, grunting. He put all of his strength into pulling on the slab but it didn't give even a half an inch.

He released it, stepped back, and shook his head. "Damn."

"That's it, then, isn't it?" Pearl said with another deep sigh.

A cracking sound emanated from the ceiling above Yakima.

He looked up at the slab again. "Hmm."

Again, he poked his fingers into the crack, got another grip on the slab, and pulled. He put all of his weight into it, bending his knees and lifting his feet up off the floor. When it didn't give, he sucked a sharp breath through gritted teeth and raised his left, wounded arm and stuck those fingers into the crack, too. He'd likely open up the wound, but if he and Pearl didn't get out of here, they were dead for sure.

He grunted, groaned, hanging all of his weight from the slab. His left arm felt like an exposed nerve. Sweat popped out on his forehead and ran down his face.

"Oh, Yakima..."

A stony crackling sounded from around the slab.

"Come on, you bastard!" Yakima grunted.

Pearl screamed and Yakima yelped with a start when the slab dropped out of the ceiling with rocks raining down around it. Yakima landed on top of it and lay stunned, staring down at it, the wind knocked out of him, his wounded arm throbbing miserably.

Raking air back into his lungs and grunting at the misery in his head, his midsection, his branded thigh as well as his arm, he rolled over to gape up at the large, round hole in the ceiling. Sure enough, it let into a large, cave-like flue trailing up through the mountain at an easy slant, leading all the way to the sky.

Pearl came over to stare up at it, eyes wide. She gasped and slapped her hands over her mouth then jumped up and down and threw herself on Yakima, hugging and kissing him.

"You broke the mountain, you big handsome devil! You broke the mountain and gave us a way out!"

Yakima stared up at the hole. And at the sky beyond the hole. He'd started wondering if he'd ever see that sky again.

"I'll be hanged," he said, glancing at the debris around him, pain sweat still dribbling down his cheeks.

She kissed his cheek then rose and extended her hand to him and helped him climb to his feet. Yakima bent forward, hands on his knees, and drew another breath into his pain-pinched lungs.

"Come on, Yakima—stop horsin' around! Let's get outta here!"

Yakima chuckled. "All right, all right. Here. You first." He dropped to one knee and patted the other one. "This is a footstool, darlin'."

"Thank you, kind sir."

Pearl placed her boot on his knee and leaped up and thrust her hands and arms into the hole in the ceiling and squirmed and wriggled until she finally drew her legs up into the flue.

"Hurry!"

Yakima looked at the opening. "Oh, Lordy."

He had to use both hands again. This might kill him. But staying down here definitely would. What a painful damned miserable life...

"All right. Step back, darlin'."

Pearl stepped back away from the hole. Yakima bent his knees and then leaped up and snaked his arms through the hole, finding purchase with his elbows. He grunted, lifting himself, using his elbows to hoist his legs up into the chasm. He was afraid he'd pass out from the pain in his arm before he rolled onto his back and away from the hole, clutching his wounded arm, which was bleeding again, and cursing under his breath.

He sweated and shuddered with the misery.

"Oh, Yakima!" Pearl knelt beside him and swabbed the sweat from his face with her shirtsleeves.

"Just a little worse for the wear, darlin'," he said, gritting his teeth against the pain and taking long, deep, even breaths. "Just a little worse for the wear..."

Finally, still shuddering a little from the pain, he heaved himself to his feet and looked around, glad to find that the slope of the flue was as gentle as it had appeared from inside the mine. Climbing out of here would be no harder than climbing your average river embankment.

Yakima held his right hand out to Pearl. "Shall we?"

"We shall!" Pearl took his hand.

He led her over to the base of the wall, and they started climbing side by side. It was just steep enough that they had to bend forward and use their hands to steady themselves, but they still made fast time and in only a few minutes they both rose up through the circular opening, stepped up onto the top of the mountain and were breathing fresh air again.

***

Renee checked her horse down in front of the Wooden Nickel Saloon in Lone Pine and glanced at her last two remaining ranch hands, McGowan and Jed Learner.

"Drinks on me, boys," she said, tonelessly.

McGowan looked back at her with his weary, pain-bright eyes. "Gonna join us, boss?"

Renee shook her head as she gazed off toward the wood-frame doctor's office. "Later."

She booted her horse on down the street and reined up in front of the white-framed building bearing the shingle of Dr. Luis Dragoman. She swung down, looped her reins over the hitchrack, mounted the boardwalk, knocked once on the glass-paned door, and stepped inside. The doctor sat at his desk, a pair of reading glasses hanging low on his nose.

Renee looked at him.

He looked back at her, skeptically, and canted his head to indicate a curtained doorway in the wall behind him. Renee strode around the desk, pushed through the curtain, and stepped into the short hall where the doctor kept two hospital rooms for overnight patients.

"On the left," the doctor called softly from his office.

Renee stopped at the door on the left. She looked at the panel, drew a breath, then tapped on it twice with her knuckles.

"Come," said Beatriz's voice.

Renee stepped into the room. Beatriz lay on the double bed to the right, her long, dark-brown hair fanned out on the crisp, white pillow. She looked pale, drawn, and sad-eyed as she turned her head to regard Renee, who softly closed the door behind her.

Renee turned to her.

Neither woman said anything for a full minute.

Then Renee stepped forward, placed her hand on the brass post at the foot of the bed. "It's finished."

Beatriz just looked at her through those soft, dark eyes. She tucked her bottom lip under her upper teeth then pushed it back out again, keeping her gaze on Renee.

"Were you in love with him?" Renee asked.

The question seemed to have caught Beatriz off guard. She frowned as though pondering her answer and, finding it, finding herself surprised by it. "Yes."

"He had to die. He killed my son."

"What happened to you, Renee? How did you get like this? Your heart is a black thing."

"You know what happened?" Renee said. "It happened to both of us."

"It was a long time ago."

"It's a brand you wear forever. Being found out…being punished so savagely. I found salvation in Daniel. And you took him from me."

"It wasn't Daniel I wanted."

"I know that," Renee said, her voice hard and bitter.

She stared back at her old lover.

In a way, they were still lovers, locked in a twisted embrace for as long as they both shall live.

"Anyway," Renee said, drawing a breath, "it's been a long few days. I need a drink."

She turned and walked to the door. As she placed her hand on the knob, Beatriz said, "I thought I would love you always, Renee. There was a time when I thought there was nothing you could do to make me stop loving you. But this did it."

Renee stared down at the doorknob, nodded slowly. She turned to Beatriz. "Good."

She opened the door, went out, crossed the doctor's office, and stepped outside.

She untied her reins from the hitchrack, stepped into her saddle, and rode back over to the Wooden Nickel, putting her horse up to the rack beside McGowan's mount. She looped the reins over the rack and stepped up onto the boardwalk. Something moving on the street caught the corner of her left eye and she turned to see what it was.

She gasped, mouth opening, eyes widening.

The half-breed and the marshal's daughter were riding down the street side by side. Both stared expressionlessly back at Renee. The breed's left arm was in a belt sling.

Renee blinked her eyes as though to clear them. Surely, she was seeing ghosts.

But, no...

Her heart thudded.

Yakima and the girl rode on past her. She heard him say, "Go on home, Pearl," then reined up at a saloon on the opposite side of the street from the Wooden Nickel.

He stepped down from his stallion's back, looped his reins over the rack, and stepped up onto the boardwalk. He did not look back at Renee but only pushed through the batwings and was gone.

Renee's heart thudded painfully. What was he up to?

Toying with her?

Making her wait for it?

She hurried into the Wooden Nickel. "McGowan!"

Epilogue

Yakima stood bellied up to the bar in the Rawhider Saloon, sipping a beer and a shot of whiskey. He'd likely down a whole bottle of the busthead to kill the sundry misery in his battered, branded body.

He spied movement behind him in the back bar mirror. He removed his hand from his glass and turned to see Renee's former foreman, McGowan, and a tall, long-haired, dull-eyed man in a funnel-brimmed black hat push through the batwings and stop in front of them.

Yakima recognized the long-haired man as one of the two who'd roped him back at the Bear Track headquarters.

Both men stood facing Yakima, thumbs hooked behind their cartridge belts.

Like Yakima's, McGowan's left arm was in a sling. His shirt over his left shoulder was blood-stained. The foreman looked pale and haggard, weary-eyed, resigned.

The other man, long-nosed, sharp-featured, sun-burned, looked a little apprehensive. He had good reason. Most of the Bear Track bunkhouse—everyone but him, in fact—was pushing up daisies.

Yakima didn't say anything.

He waited, staring back at the two men before him.

"She wants us to finish it," McGowan said at last.

"Dyin' is a helluva way to finish it."

The other man slid his nervous eyes toward McGowan and quickly ran his tongue across his lower lip.

McGowan frowned, canted his head a little to one side. "Are *you* finished?" His expression turned skeptical.

Yakima shrugged a shoulder. "I reckon I've killed enough of you sons of bitches."

"Really?"

"Really."

"What about her?"

"She's sick."

"Did you burn her out?"

"No." Yakima wasn't sure why, but he hadn't been able to follow through with that part of his threat even after she'd damn near buried him and Pearl alive. He felt as worn out and hollowed out as the foreman did. He'd had to exact revenge, of course, but he'd had enough. And to be honest, it didn't make him feel much better.

He was still branded.

McGowan and the other man gazed skeptically back at Yakima.

"Get out of here," Yakima said. "Don't ever let me see either one of you again."

McGowan gazed back at him. He turned to the other man and then McGowan backed through the batwings, keeping his hand near his six-shooter. The other man followed suit, and they were gone, batwings clattering into place behind them.

Yakima sighed, sipped his beer.

He'd taken several more sips and was staring into his beer, pondering what had happened here over the past several days, when something red flashed in the backbar mirror before him.

He wheeled just as Renee Stratton burst through the batwings, her eyes nearly as red as her hair, and brought up a cocked six-shooter. She aimed it at Yakima and stretched her lips back from her teeth.

The gun thundered.

Yakima flinched, for she had him dead to rights. Only...it wasn't Renee's gun that had spoken. It was a gun behind her.

Renee's arm dropped and her hand opened. Her gun clunked to the floor.

Renee took two stumbling steps forward, staring at Yakima now with an expression of deep disbelief, her eyes wide, her lips twisted.

She took another halting step forward. Her gaze slid to the backbar mirror and acquired a sad, disappointed cast.

She fell to the floor. Blood oozed from the hole in her back, between her shoulder blades.

Just beyond the batwings, McGowan stood holding a Colt revolver straight out from his right shoulder. Smoke curled from the barrel.

His stricken gaze on Renee, he slowly lowered the gun. He holstered it, strode heavily through the batwings, crouched, grabbed one of Renee's limp hands with his own right one, and drew her up over his good shoulder. He did not look at Yakima. He turned and strode back out through the batwings with the dead woman in his arms.

Renee's red hair dangled down over the backs of his legs.

The batwings clattered into place behind him but soon swung open again as Pearl ran through them. She stopped, gazed in horror at Yakima. Then, her gaze turning to relief, she ran to him and slammed her body against his, hugging him tightly, breathing hard.

Yakima groaned against the assault. He wrapped his good arm around her.

He could feel her heart beating against his chest.

She looked up at him. "Is it over?"

Yakima nodded. "It's over."

A Look At: Shotgun Rider: A Western Double

Meet Dag Enberg, a brand-new western hero from the author of the Sherriff Ben Stillman Westerns, Peter Brandvold – king of the gritty, sexy, hard-driving western!

In this violent, sexy western double, Dag Enberg is a shotgun rider for Arizona's Yuma Stage Line. When a group of outlaws led by Cougar Ketchum kidnap Enberg's pregnant wife and threaten to kill her if Enberg doesn't turn over a valuable strongbox, Enberg is forced to go against his instincts. He turns over the box without a fight.

The owner of the strongbox, Logan Cates, believes that Enberg has thrown in with Ketchum. When Cates turns his sites on the shotgun rider, a bloody war breaks out . . . as well as a desperate chase into Mexico for the stolen gold and Enberg's woman.

For a while, Dag Enberg manages to hold onto his job as shotgun rider for the Yuma Line. He soon returns to his old brawling ways, however, and gets himself fired when he raises a drunken ruckus in a saloon and beds the beautiful . . . and off-limits . . . Zenobia Chevere.

AVAILABLE NOW

ABOUT THE AUTHOR

Peter Brandvold grew up in the great state of North Dakota in the 1960's and '70s, when television westerns were as popular as shows about hoarders and shark tanks are now, and western paperbacks were as popular as Game of Thrones.

Brandvold watched every western series on television at the time. He grew up riding horses and herding cows on the farms of his grandfather and many friends who owned livestock.

Brandvold's imagination has always lived and will always live in the West. He is the author of over a hundred lightning-fast action westerns under his own name and his pen name, Frank Leslie.

CPSIA information can be obtained
at www.ICGtesting.com
Printed in the USA
LVHW040905081221
705576LV00004B/369

9 781647 346287